IS THIS SUITCASE TAKEN?

SWEETFERN HARBOR MYSTERY #13

WENDY MEADOWS

MAJESTIC OWL WL PUBLISHING LLC

1

THE WEDDING

Large bouquets of hibiscus and bird-of-paradise flowers arrived at Sheffield Bed and Breakfast in colorful sprays of tropical glamor. Brenda Rivers gasped at the beauty that would adorn the main table where her father and his new bride would sit after pronouncing their wedding vows. The day would represent the culmination of months of meticulous planning by Brenda, Phyllis and Allie. Her head housekeeper and good friend Phyllis was as excited as Brenda's young reservationist Allie. Allie created the décor for the banquet and guest tables, and as the flower displays were carried inside, Allie was busy setting tiki torches into the lawn on either side of the walkway leading to the garden where the ceremony would take place.

"Everything looks perfect. That centerpiece is just beautiful, Jenny," Brenda said. "You have outdone yourself this time." The owner of Jenny's Blossoms had just arrived bearing the main bouquet.

Jenny Jones beamed. "Your father and Morgan deserve only the best, Brenda. I selected flowers for the wedding from my research about Hawaii and I do feel the choices are perfect. These were flown in from Florida just this morning, believe it or not."

"What about the loose orchid petals?" Phyllis said. "Did you get enough?"

Jenny laughed. "Of course, I did, Phyllis. There is nothing to worry about. The guest list is not too big, so there will be plenty of petals for everyone to shower down on the bride and groom."

After her stepdaughter left to retrieve more arrangements from her flower shop, Brenda looked at the invoice and did not even balk at the cost. Her father deserved the best, and she had no problem with extravagance. For such an intimate wedding, every detail had to be perfect. The large Queen Anne house would be lit and decorated for the banquet reception, the porches and terraces with twinkling lights and garlands of tropical flowers echoing the overall theme, and the garden ceremony would take place under a canopy of trailing vines and billowing, gauzy linen.

"Did you convince your father to wear a Hawaiian-themed wedding suit, Brenda?" Phyllis's tone held humor. "Are we going to see color on Tim or just his standard black and white and gray?"

"He agreed to wear a white jacket and to wear the leafy vine lei. I think that's a lot for him."

The women laughed, remembering how Tim Sheffield

and Morgan Graber had insisted on a small wedding. The three women, once planning began, found it hard to hold back. The couple let it slip eventually that they planned to honeymoon in Hawaii and that was all it took for Brenda, Phyllis and Allie to plan the theme and a big splash for the reception afterwards.

"I almost forgot, Phyllis. Our seashell leis are at Jenny's shop. She will bring them over along with Morgan's orchid lei and Dad's maile-vine lei, fresh right before the ceremony. Everything will be perfect."

"I'll call Molly to check if she needs help in her back kitchen."

After a quick call, Phyllis asked Allie if she wanted to go down with her. Allie said her new guests would be arriving at any moment. Brenda began to pace as all their plans began to clash together at the last moment. Then Allie reassured her check-in would go smooth as usual, and Phyllis convinced her to expend her energies and accompany her to Morning Sun Coffee instead. With so much to do for the wedding catering, Phyllis's daughter had hired extra help to take care of her coffee shop customers and had been busy in her catering kitchen behind the coffee shop for days.

Phyllis and Brenda entered through the back door of Morning Sun Coffee, right into the catering kitchen. Molly greeted them with a wave of her hand while she chopped pineapple slices into chunks. She wasted no time getting down to business.

"Do you want the pineapple on skewers, Brenda? I know there was some back and forth on how to serve the tropical fruits." Brenda agreed that skewers were best. At

Molly's instruction, she and Phyllis washed their hands and donned aprons to cut more fruit into colorful wedges. Meanwhile Molly, notebook in hand, walked around her large kitchen and checked tasks off a lengthy list. As she chopped, Brenda peeped around in wonder. "I can't thank everyone enough for pitching in to make my dad's wedding a Hawaiian dream come true. It's like everyone in Sweetfern Harbor is involved."

"We know how much this means to your dad, Brenda. Besides, you're family," Phyllis insisted, wiping her hands on her apron.

It wasn't long before Brenda and Phyllis finished the fruit cutting work. They washed up and bid Molly goodbye and good luck with the rest of her work and set out to return to the bed and breakfast.

Hope Williams, the baker, called Brenda's mobile phone as the women walked up the slight hill to the mansion. Hope was on her way to Sheffield Bed and Breakfast to deliver the wedding cake and other morsels she'd concocted for the occasion. Sweet Treats never failed to deliver perfect baked goods, and Brenda could not wait to see everything. "See you soon, Hope! My mouth is already watering," said Brenda.

When Brenda and Phyllis walked up to the front door of Sheffield House, Brenda noted her husband standing at the edge of the side lawn and waved gaily to him. William Pendleton, Phyllis's husband, stood by Mac admiring the rose garden and waved down to his own wife with a fond smile.

Mac Rivers stood with his hands on his hips and shook his head slightly. William Pendleton chuckled. "What did I tell you, Detective?" he said. "Our wives simply can't restrain themselves."

"I suppose we have to hand it to them for at least keeping the guest list small like Morgan and Tim requested." He glanced at the sky. "It's a beautiful day for a wedding. I'm happy for the couple. Morgan has no plans to continue working here, according to Brenda, but I'm not so sure…I think she will ultimately fool all of us."

Brenda walked up to Mac. "What do you think so far?" She gestured to the tiki torches and garlands lining the garden path to the ceremony location.

"So far? Do you mean there's going to be more?"

"The food preparation is underway, and Jenny has more flowers to bring over. Allie is putting together smaller coconut and pineapple centerpieces for the tables. Dad and Morgan's table will have a more elaborate centerpiece, but they will be able to see over it. It's in our walk-in right now…"

Mac kissed his wife on the cheek. "It's beautiful, Brenda. I don't need every detail. I'm sure everything you've put together will be perfect."

As Allie checked guests in, she told them of the wedding on the premises later that afternoon. Although it was intended to be a small wedding, rather than shut anyone out, they had decided to invite all the guests even though they didn't know the couple.

"Dickinsons, checking in," a male voice said cheerily, stepping up to the counter after the first group had checked in. "We are here for the wedding." Shane Dickinson told Allie they were long-time friends of Tim Sheffield. He and his wife Sandra were from Michigan.

"We have never met Tim's daughter Brenda but have heard a lot about her. Tim often told us how proud he is of her."

Allie called Brenda to tell her of the guests' arrival. Brenda came out and gave them a warm welcome and invited everyone for refreshments in the sitting room where they could become better acquainted.

Allie's eyes lit on a couple arriving just then who appeared to be in their mid-forties. Carrie Porter and Rick Dawson smiled at her as they checked in and chatted amiably. Michael the porter came to carry their bags to their room on the second floor. He and Allie exchanged glances when they saw the very large black suitcase the couple had brought inside. Carrie had two overnight bags plus a normal-sized rolling suitcase. Rick pulled another suitcase along and picked up his overnight case. Luckily for Michael, the huge one was also on rollers.

Allie had little time to wonder why someone would carry in so much luggage for a four-day stay. She was distracted when Daniel Swift appeared before her. His friendly smile and charming demeanor drew Allie in. He told her he was taking advantage of the weekend to get away from his car dealership. Daniel explained he spent too much time there and the only way to escape was to leave town completely. He complimented Allie's eyes and handed her his business card before he walked off to find his room.

A half hour passed with no new guests until a woman walked in. Her eyes darted from side to side as she stopped and took in the grandeur of the 1890s Queen Anne architecture. She had dark brown hair and amber eyes. Her frame was slender, and Allie thought she would be more attractive if she held her head up rather than hunched downward as she took in her surroundings. Allie welcomed her cheerfully, and the woman's weak smile returned.

"I'm Alexandra Cornell," she said. "I have a reservation for the next few days."

"You are on my list," Allie said. She told Alexandra about Sweetfern Harbor and the many specialty shops it was known for as she checked the woman in. "If you like to walk by the water, the ocean is at the bottom of that pathway behind the seawall. There is a wonderful beach area." Alexandra nodded her head without speaking. "We have a Hawaiian-themed wedding that will take place on the side lawn at four this afternoon. Our guests are welcome to attend."

Alexandra nodded again. Michael retrieved the woman's two large suitcases and Alexandra slung the strap of her overnight case over her shoulder. Behind her back, Allie shook her head wonderingly at Michael. This weekend, the guests all seemed to have over-packed.

"You really should pull your hair back, young lady. All those curls, why don't you try a bun? Don't hide that beautiful face." The presumptuous voice came from a middle-aged man who walked rapidly toward the front desk. "Some sophistication would do you wonders." He extended his hand forcefully. "I'm Patrick Anderson. Nice to meet you. I don't suppose you can give me any information about where to find a good sailing instructor in town?"

"I'm just the reservationist." Allie attempted to

maintain her pleasant demeanor, but she took an instant dislike toward the guest who had so rudely greeted her. "You might try Jonathan Wright's boat rental business. He teaches water sports." She handed him one of Jon's business cards.

Michael noted her muted agitation and stepped forward to take Patrick's bags. "I hope I'm not going to be stashed in some back room with a view of the parking lot," Patrick said, leaning forward into Allie's space. "I don't care for that kind of treatment, and I'm not afraid to complain to the manager."

"All of our rooms have great views and are airy and open," Michael said, trying to rescue Allie. The guest did not seem to take the hint and looked around the entry hallway with a skeptical expression. He finally followed Michael when the porter took the two largest bags and started for the stairs.

Allie didn't give Patrick Anderson any more information – not even a mention of the refreshments in the sitting room available for newly-arrived guests. She seethed at his rude comment. She was young, yes, but did that give him a right to tell her how she should wear her hair? Allie was artistic and creative, not the type to aim for sophistication, no matter what a stranger might say.

Phyllis had been dusting the small alcove a few paces away from the front desk. She'd overheard the exchange. "Don't pay any attention to him, Allie. People who talk and act like that are insecure, in my estimation."

Allie took a deep breath. "I can't believe I let him get to me like that."

"Forget him. We have a wedding today."

Brenda and Mac had been asked to serve as matron of honor and best man. Phyllis and William were the only other attendants for the wedding. Allie and the other employees, along with Molly, Hope and Jenny, would make sure all wedding guests were served well.

Brenda hurried to her cottage with Mac after the Dickinsons and other guests had been shown to their room. They showered and dressed for the big event. Brenda felt overjoyed that her father had recovered from her mother's death and found someone new in his life. He planned to travel in his retirement but always hesitated, lacking a companion. Morgan longed to travel and so far had had little time to do so. Brenda didn't blame Morgan for planning to leave Sheffield Bed and Breakfast as head chef. She had given Brenda a month's notice. If the temporary chef Brenda had hired for the wedding and honeymoon worked out, Brenda planned to offer him the job. But first, she also wanted to make sure Morgan was serious about wanting to quit.

Brenda smoothed down her dress, a jewel-colored sheathe with a spray of Hawaiian blooms embroidered in glittering thread along the shoulders. As she admired her dress in the mirror, Mac walked up behind her. "You look incredible," he said, fastening the seashell lei around her neck. "Even more beautiful than the day we married." Mac dropped a soft kiss onto the top of her head and together they walked downstairs to join everyone in the side garden.

On their way to the back door, they passed Hope Williams and her husband, local news anchorman David Williams. The Williamses carefully carried in the wedding cake to wait in the kitchen for the reception. The cake towered with three tiers of glittering sugar and flowers, each layer iced with bright tropical colors. On top, a couple wearing Hawaiian leis gazed at one another, holding hands. Brenda complimented Hope on once again astonishing them all with her baking expertise.

Out in the garden, the wedding attendants stood together on the stone terrace, looking across at the mingling guests and waiting for their cue for the ceremony to begin. "I haven't heard from the ukulele player this afternoon," Brenda fretted. "I hope he hasn't forgotten."

Phyllis laughed at her. "He called this morning, Brenda. Try to enjoy yourself, and quit worrying about things going wrong."

Brenda smiled. "You're right. I'll just enjoy it like everyone else. Are all of the bed and breakfast guests planning to attend?"

"Allie told me several opted out, but it was kind of last minute, I suppose. Rick Dawson and Carrie Porter apparently don't believe in marriage, whatever that means. Probably they just wanted to go downtown alone. In any case, they were polite to Allie. I don't believe Daniel Swift plans to come, either. He told Allie he appreciated the invitation, but he wanted to take a walk down along the beach. Allie told me he was a bit of a flirt, actually, but I told her not to get carried away – the man's a salesman, so he can probably flirt with anything that moves, as long as he might make a sale. He's here to get away from his busy life as a car dealership manager, according to her."

Just then, Phyllis pointed across the lawn, where the ukulele player waved to them. His name was Ben and he had driven in from several towns over. Ben made his living performing solo and with bands at weddings and small concerts, and he had a lovely repertoire of classic Hawaiian tunes. Ben took his spot at the side of the wedding canopy.

Everything waited in readiness and the afternoon sun shone down, gleaming golden on everyone's finery. It was time for the ceremony to begin.

Phyllis and Brenda stood at the start of the pathway to the arbor, between the tiki torches garlanded with flowers. The ukulele player began the Hawaiian Wedding Song. Brenda and Phyllis, and then Mac and William, processed down the pathway to stand at the arch awaiting the bride. When Brenda reached the arch, she stood on her tiptoes to kiss her father's cheek, and he nearly teared up in happiness, his normally serious expression full of emotion. He stood in his fine linen suit, his hands clasped before him, his eyes glued to the doorway where his bride would appear. Everyone turned in anticipation, peering across the fragrant garden.

Morgan took a deep breath. Her brother, Amos, escorted her out the door and down to the lawn between the tiki torches. Morgan's heart overflowed when she met Tim's eyes. When they stopped under the arbor laden with colorful flowers and leafy green garlands, Amos whispered in her ear how happy he was that Morgan found a good man. She fought tears and moved forward next to her soon-to-be husband.

Brenda, too, swallowed several times during the ceremony to keep the lump in her throat down. She squeezed Mac's hand when the officiant read the vows, which instantly reminded Brenda of their own wedding not so long ago.

After the groom kissed his bride, a great cheer went up among the guests, and the newly married couple swung their joined hands on the way back through the garden area while the guests tossed fragrant orchid petals over them. Tim tenderly held Morgan's hand as she stepped into a white limo and then they were driven throughout Sweetfern Harbor with the windows down. Everyone in town stood along the main street and waved and cheered.

By the time the couple returned to Sheffield Bed and Breakfast, everything waited in readiness for the banquet. The new couple was escorted to the sweetheart table at the front of the room with the wedding cake posed in the background. Plates heaped with delicious food from the Hawaiian-themed banquet were set before them.

"Brenda, everything is so beautiful," Morgan said when they finally had a chance to chat amid the happy talk and music and picture-taking. "There are no words for how perfect it all turned out. Thank you from the bottom of our hearts." Tim echoed his appreciation and his eyes shone in the dimming late-afternoon sunlight. He had eyes only for his new bride, who he cradled in the circle of his arm the whole time.

"I am so glad you approve, but we're not finished yet. The big celebration is yet to come," Brenda teased.

Phyllis and Allie waved to the ukulele player, who ended the dance tune with a flourish so Mac could stand up and call for a toast. He asked everyone to lift their drinks to the happy couple. "Tim and Morgan, I'm so happy for you. You show us that love and marriage can surprise us at any age. Here's to years and years of adventures together. To love, no matter when it finds us… to family, no matter where we find it…and to home, no matter where we make it." The audience cheered.

"We'll take a break for a while and then the main dinner will be served." He pointed to the dance floor. "Be prepared to shake a leg tonight." He thanked Ben, the ukulele player, after introducing him. The guests clapped and some stuck around talking and others dispersed to recoup.

"The early fall temperature is so refreshing," Sandra Dickinson said when she came around to congratulate Brenda and her father. "Perfect for a wedding. I can see why you decided to move out this way. No wonder your father was convinced to join you here! There's something special about the ocean air."

Brenda discussed how happy they both were with their choice. "My uncle Randolph was very generous in leaving the bed and breakfast to me. If that hadn't happened, I would never have met Mac Rivers and Dad wouldn't be so happy today with Morgan. I think it was meant to be."

They chatted for a while and Brenda introduced Sandra and Shane to her friends and other guests. Then she excused herself when she saw Mac and David step out into the hall and return with heaping platters of food. The others followed suit and helped bring the catered dishes out to the tables.

"Nothing can possibly mar such a wonderful day," Hope said. She walked with Brenda as they carried trays of skewered fruits. "I love this theme. I can't get enough of this pineapple," she said and grabbed another skewer of the mouth-watering tropical fruit.

Brenda beamed. Everyone enjoyed the delicious lomi-lomi salmon and mochiko chicken served with fragrant side dishes of gingered sweet potatoes and a colorful coleslaw. Cilantro lime rice and Thai curried beef completed the main course options.

"It's too bad some of the bed and breakfast guests are missing this celebration. I didn't expect to be welcomed like this," Alexandra Cornell said, peering up from her plate. "I wonder where Daniel is. Have you seen him?" The guest near her had no idea who Daniel was and when Alexandra explained he was another guest, the woman guessed he may be walking along the beach. Brenda was surprised she said so much. Since her arrival, Alexandra had spoken little and clearly felt timid in such a crowd.

Allie pulled Brenda aside some minutes later as they were refilling their cups with sparkling fruit punch. "I didn't think Alexandra knew anyone here," she said.

"Apparently she knows Daniel. I suppose she's talking about Daniel Swift."

Allie smiled. "Maybe she just thinks he's cute? Maybe he's been flirting with her, too." Allie rolled her eyes.

The party was in full swing when Morgan and Tim began to circle the room hand in hand, mingling with the crowd and ensuring they thanked every guest for coming. They stopped in front of Brenda and Phyllis and expressed their happiness at the hard work the women had done to pull it all off.

"We're leaving now," Tim said. "We'll drive to New York and spend the night. Our flight leaves for Hawaii around noon tomorrow. Thank you, Brenda." He hugged his daughter and she congratulated him again.

After they left, Brenda searched for Mac. She was ready to dance again. She spotted him away from the crowd on his phone. The look on his face told Brenda he probably would not stick around for the party. She was right. He approached her with an unsettled look on his face.

"What is it, Mac?"

"Bryce left the party to go back and man the station for a while. He called and said some officers reported hearing a noise at the rear door. They thought it was a raccoon knocking over boxes in the dumpster. When one of the officers went to check, he found a large black suitcase of some kind wedged back there." Mac looked around at the group of happy revelers with an anxious look. "Where's Jenny? Bryce is worried about her going back home alone. She's almost ready to have that baby. Convince her to stay here tonight so he won't have to worry."

"She can stay in one of the guest rooms in our cottage, Mac. I'll find her. What's the matter? You look like you saw a ghost. What was in the suitcase?"

Mac hesitated before leaning in close to her ear to tell her the grisly details. "They found a dead body in it when they opened it. The man hadn't been dead for very long. They are taking DNA evidence and other things now to determine his identity."

Phyllis, Allie, Hope and Molly watched the couple in their serious conversation.

"What's going on?" Jonathan said. The boat rental owner put his arm around Molly's shoulders. "I was hoping we could have this next dance."

"I'll be happy to dance with you and only you, Jon, but we're curious about what's going on between Brenda and Mac. It looks like there's something serious afoot. Maybe we need to end the party a little early."

Brenda parted with Mac and knew she would have to tell her friends something. She swallowed and looked around. No one else was aware of anything amiss. To their expectant faces, she said only, "There is a situation at the police station...a body needs to be identified. That's all I know. Have any of you seen Jenny? Bryce will be busy all night down there and he doesn't want her going home alone."

Allie pointed across the room where Jenny danced, the dress on her bulging stomach twirling out, its pink bow fluttering in the air. "Baby bump first. That's how I find her these days." She grinned and waved for Jenny to join them when she caught her eye.

Jenny often spent a night in the cottage guest room when Bryce worked late nights, and the girls had been up chatting late into the night. Brenda and her young daughter-in-law had become closer than ever over time, and it comforted them both to have Jenny sleeping close by someone else in case the baby made an early appearance.

"I don't want any of the guests to be alarmed. Perhaps...Phyllis, will you tell Ben the ukulele player that we're all done for the night? Without music I think folks will start to head home or up to their rooms," Brenda said.

Phyllis quickly got to work and everyone else began to clear the tables. As Ben ended his last song and thanked the enthusiastic little crowd, a number of the guests started to pick up their jackets and bid everyone goodnight. Soon the dining room space was nearly empty.

Phyllis and William walked Jenny and Brenda over to the cottage Brenda and Mac called home. It seemed terrible luck for a wedding to end like this, and Brenda tried to convince herself it was merely a coincidence.

"No matter what's going on over at the police station, you can rest easy tonight, Brenda," William said as they walked. "At least your father left town without ever knowing that something had happened. He and Morgan were so happy tonight."

"You're right," Brenda said, but her mind remained troubled. "I just want to know…why would anyone dump a dead body right at the door of a police station?" Phyllis and Jenny nodded, thinking.

Brenda had no answer.

2

THE DEAD BODY

Daniel Swift could not believe his eyes when he saw Alexandra Cornell in the sitting room at Sheffield Bed and Breakfast. Finally, he had managed to escape the never-ending demands of his dealership business and had begun to enjoy the refreshing salt air. But he had not left his stalker behind, after all.

Daniel and Alexandra dated for only two months when they were in college. That was almost two decades ago. Since the breakup, Alexandra made sure she knew his every move. More than once, he'd sensed her eyes on him if he went out with another woman.

He had yet to determine how she knew he'd planned a getaway along the Atlantic Ocean in this quaint little town, and specifically at the Sheffield Bed and Breakfast. His anxiety heightened every time he was forced to avoid her. That was no easy task. The Queen Anne mansion, though large, had hallways and rooms that connected. Alexandra appeared around every corner.

When Daniel confirmed that Alexandra planned to attend the wedding, he breathed a sigh of relief, knowing he had most of the day free without having to dodge her. He set out as soon as he could in the morning for the bracing salt air of the beach, walking along the pebbly surface.

"I can't believe it's you, Daniel," a familiar voice called after him. "What in the world are you doing up in Sweetfern Harbor? I didn't think you liked small towns and anonymity like this."

Patrick Anderson still had the same cocky mannerisms Daniel remembered well. His first inclination was to act as if he didn't recognize Patrick, but he knew that was a hopeless approach.

"I get away at times," he smiled gamely.

"What did you do with that college degree?" Patrick cocked his head sideways. "You did graduate in the end, right? I hope you've made it big." The scowl and anger on Daniel's face would have stopped the most blatant questions of most people, but Patrick read him like a book and laughed. "I guess you ended up back in that rundown town you came from, am I right?"

"I'm a successful businessman, in spite of your wasted attempts to cause failure to rain down upon my life. You didn't win, Patrick."

Daniel realized his old acquaintance was not only going to be unpleasant, but downright combative, so he walked toward the sandy area away from the small pebbles and away from Patrick Anderson. He heard the low chuckle that escaped Patrick's mouth. Daniel felt he had two options now that two of the people he despised most in life would be sharing close quarters with him at the bed and breakfast. He could pack up and leave early or he could make sure he avoided them as much as possible.

There was another option he could consider but it would be risky. He watched the sailboats to calm himself and became intrigued with the seagulls. He studied their dipping and swerving along the rollicking winds to feed from the waves. Each bird carried out a single-minded purpose to remain free. He would have to seek the same single-mindedness himself.

Alexandra Cornell found it impossible to release her feelings for Daniel Swift. Even after twenty years had passed since her college days, she clung to the memory of the time they had spent together. Alexandra knew that one day Daniel would realize his mistake and come back to her. She knew he had married and divorced twice; obviously she was the right one for him if the other two had proven to be disappointments. If she could convince him that she was his true love, then her life would be complete, as would his.

Daniel may try to ignore her as usual, but she knew this time it would work. How could he hope to avoid her in a quaint seaside town? How could anyone keep from falling in love with such a beautiful backdrop?

Soon after she checked into Sheffield Bed and Breakfast, Alexandra was surprised to see Patrick Anderson there, too. She had never liked him. Something happened long ago between Patrick and Daniel that left a lingering sense of sour distaste between the two men. Patrick was also part of the reason Daniel left her all those years ago. She was sure of it. Now she shuddered when she thought of Patrick's greeting to her.

"Still the mousy girl I knew in college, aren't you, Alexandra? Are you still scurrying around half-scared of your own shadow? I thought you and Daniel would be happily settled in together by now." The leer in his eyes penetrated to her soul. "I'm glad to see both of you here, in fact. Are you married or just engaged?" He continued, relentless, peering down at her finger and spying the lack of a ring. "Neither? Never fear, dear. I'm sure everything will work out between you."

The man was as obnoxious as ever. Alexandra didn't answer him and locked herself in her room as soon as she could. She had hoped Daniel would lodge in the room next to hers. Instead, she heard Patrick enter the room next door. She steamed over her plans going awry so quickly. Alexandra took a deep breath and concentrated on how to win Daniel over to her once and for all. She was nothing if not persistent. Patrick would simply be a speed bump, not a dead end.

When Alexandra dressed and went down for the wedding, she searched for Daniel, anxiously smoothing down her dress. She decided he must be coming later. Brenda Rivers had offered her a mai tai cocktail and she'd accepted, clutching the drink nervously as she eyed the growing crowd.

"What do you think of the bed and breakfast?" Brenda said. "I hope you enjoy your stay with us."

At the time, Alexandra mumbled an answer, but her

focus was on finding Daniel and not whether she liked her lodgings or not. Without thinking, she crept away from Brenda and wandered around the wedding area. Brenda trailed off mid-sentence, thinking that her guest must be quite tired and distracted; she did not like to think that Alexandra was being rude.

During the ceremony, Alexandra had taken a seat next to Sandra Dickinson. Sandra tried to strike up a conversation before the ukulele player began the entrance song, but Alexandra was frantically looking up and down the rows of seats for her quarry. Sandra gave up with a shrug when the woman didn't respond.

After the wedding, Alexandra still failed to locate Daniel. Frustrated and overwhelmed by the noise and bustle of the party, she decided to take a walk toward the seawall until dinner was served. She listened to the distant music and dreamed of planning her own wedding and going to Hawaii with Daniel one day. When she got to the seawall, she sat on the lower end of it. This gave her a view of the sandy beach below and the ocean, as well as the wedding celebrations in the garden and the house beyond. It was pretty from a distance. It was exactly the right kind of romantic setting to convince Daniel they were meant to be together. She waited, and she watched, and she knew what she needed to do.

Carrie Porter strolled down the main street of Sweetfern Harbor and searched for her boyfriend Rick. She was pleased to have avoided the wedding at their accommodations but annoyed that she could not head back there to rest. She loved Rick Dawson deeply but had long ago agreed with him that marriage would ruin everything for them. In any case, they had always been very loyal to one another, enjoying their freedom and never missing the chance to skip out on horribly boring weddings.

She hadn't seen him in over an hour and he wasn't answering his cell phone. Carrie continued strolling down the quaint street, gazing in the store windows and checking for Rick as she went. Most of the shops were open and she noted people beginning to line up along the sidewalks of the main street. It didn't take long for her to realize they were waiting to cheer the newlyweds on as they drove by in the limo.

Carrie rolled her eyes gamely. She stood in the background of the crowd, amused to see the two people in their sixties waving to the whole town after they had exchanged wedding vows. She window-shopped along the street and went inside several of them. After a few purchases, she reached Morning Sun Coffee and saw one table available near the window with a street view. She decided to sit and watch the crowds go by, and perhaps she would see Rick.

"Why are there so many people in town?" she asked the young server.

"It's a weekend, and that's when tourists come up. Other than the wedding at Sheffield Bed and Breakfast, there isn't anything special going on this weekend, but they still come." She set the latté down in front of Carrie. "Of course, the wedding was only for close friends of the couple, but it's a small town. Everybody knows everybody. We all celebrate it from a distance. As you probably noticed." Her melodious laughter caused Carrie to smile.

After another hour, Carrie gave up the waiting game and walked back toward the bed and breakfast, attempting another call to Rick. She had no idea why he wasn't answering his phone and left another message. "I had hoped we could have dinner at the Italian restaurant downtown, Rick. You like Italian. Where have you been all afternoon, anyway? Give me a call." She then told him she was on her way to Sheffield Bed and Breakfast.

The dead body found at the back door of the police station kept Brenda's mind busy. Unable to sleep, she had joined a few employees and friends continuing the cleanup at the main house. She wiped her hands on the towel and told everyone thanks again. Phyllis and William sat down at the kitchen work table. Brenda put on a fresh pot of coffee and joined them.

"I suppose you haven't gotten word yet from Mac on who the body is," William said.

Brenda shook her head. She hadn't even had time to assess which of her guests were around and who were not. She had been so busy with the wedding arrangements and the celebration, she was not even certain exactly who had attended. Brenda felt a little guilty for not paying more attention. At least by morning, she should know who spent the night in their rooms.

"More coffee, Phyllis?"

Her friend yawned with a wan smile. "We're ready to go home, Brenda. I'll do the last lock-up for you and we can all leave through the kitchen door," Phyllis said.

When Brenda arrived at the cottage, she peeked into the guest room. Jenny snored softly, and Brenda closed the door and got ready for bed. It took less than five minutes for her to fall into a deep sleep.

Brenda awakened at seven and put coffee on. The teakettle simmered on low and she placed several tea bags out for Jenny. She left a note that she would be in the dining room of the bed and breakfast and once again checked on Jenny, who began to stir and then settle back into sleep. Brenda turned the teakettle off.

When she arrived at the dining room, she noted several early risers. Carrie Porter and Rick Dawson were at the buffet filling their plates. Sandra and Shane Dickinson were enjoying their breakfast. They talked of the wedding with other guests. Carrie and Rick smiled at their enthusiasm. Sandra asked how they liked the Hawaiian theme. With amused smiles, they told her they had not attended but heard it was quite beautiful.

The night before, Carrie had been relieved when Rick finally showed up. He told her his phone had gone dead and he didn't get her messages until he charged it again. He promised to spend the entire day next with her. Sandra and Shane offered their own suggestions for sights and shops to visit.

Brenda greeted them all and sat down for a few minutes with her guests. She stayed long enough to ask if they needed anything before she joined Phyllis in the housekeeper's former apartment in the bed and breakfast.

"I think everyone is going out today, Phyllis. There will be plenty of time until early afternoon to get rooms in order for them. Sandra and Shane will be the only two here for lunch. We can join them if you'd like."

Their usual morning chat was interrupted when Brenda's cell rang. It was Mac.

"We've identified the body, Brenda. Unfortunately, it was one of our guests. Patrick Anderson. I think I mentioned the body was inside a large suitcase. Well, it is more like an over-sized footlocker. Did you see anyone come in with something like that?"

"No, but I can ask Allie what she saw. Michael carries a lot of the luggage up for the guests on arrival and departure days, so I could ask him. I think he's out of town this weekend, however," she said.

"Don't worry about that. Just ask Allie when you get time. I know you're busy with a full house, but when you get a minute, come down and I'll fill you in on the details we have so far. We'll need to question some of the guests for sure, establish a timeline."

Phyllis noted Brenda's face and presumed the caller was Mac with news of the dead body. Brenda hung up and relayed what her husband told her. "I'll go to the kitchen first and see if Chef Pierre needs anything. If you have time, Phyllis, check to see if he needs anything today. Lunch will be a small gathering, but I expect everyone will be here for dinner tonight from the list I saw."

In a few short hours, they learned Patrick's parents were traveling overseas and could not be contacted for several days. Detective Bryce Jones worked to track down a distant cousin and his wife who lived in Terre Haute, Indiana. Mac and his two officers searched for clues in the large trunk while continually being interrupted with other business at hand. The weekend proved an active one as several domestic issues were reported from around town.

At lunchtime, Brenda greeted her two guests, and she and Phyllis sat down with them. Servers served each of them, and Chef Pierre's rotisserie chicken salad with grapes and walnuts hit the spot with the diners.

"I envy your father and Morgan, Brenda," Sandra said. "I know how much they will enjoy Hawaii. We were there several years ago and have wanted to go back ever since."

Brenda was relieved to talk about Hawaii. So far, these guests had no idea someone they'd met at Sheffield Bed and Breakfast the day before had been dropped off at the Sweetfern Harbor police station, dead. She was anxious to get back down to the investigation with her husband. At the same time, Brenda enjoyed carrying on her hostess duties as if nothing was amiss.

After lunch, she joined Allie at the front desk. Her young receptionist's head was buried in a textbook. She looked up when Brenda approached.

"I've got one more test this week," Allie said. "That should be the last until after Christmas, and I'll be so glad."

They discussed Allie's college ambitions. She had aced all of her exams this year so far and Brenda had no doubt she would do the same with this one. They went over the guest roster together and Allie pointed out several special requests a few guests had mentioned.

"No one has asked for anything we can't provide, thankfully. I don't like it when someone arrives and expects special services like a high-end hotel in Europe or some place."

Brenda laughed. "If they do, let's see if we can match that concept. Who has asked for special attention?"

"Carrie Porter asked for a first aid kit, which I gave her. It's a good thing we keep things like that ready. She's a nurse, so I suppose she felt helpless without it. Then there was Patrick Anderson, who asked for a blank journal to write in. That was last night before I left for home. He was offended he didn't get one in his room." Allie rolled her eyes. "I'm sorry, Brenda…I just wanted to get rid of him as soon as possible. He's hopelessly rude. I saw Alexandra speaking with Rick Dawson and his girlfriend Carrie, but none of them have asked for anything."

Brenda reminded her to be patient with everyone. She didn't feel it was the time to tell Allie that Patrick Anderson would not be bothering her again. Brenda decided to go into Patrick's room and look for his recently acquired journal. For the sake of a witness, she asked Phyllis to go upstairs with her to his room.

"What are we looking for?" Phyllis asked. She closed the door behind them. Brenda handed her a pair of latex gloves.

"Look for a journal or anything in Patrick's handwriting."

Brenda called Mac to tell him what they were doing.

"That's a good idea, Brenda. I'm sending two plainclothes officers over there. Meet them at the back door. They'll do a thorough search of his room that may tell us why someone wanted to kill the man."

After the call, Phyllis offered to wait on the back patio for the officers and bring them upstairs. Brenda continued to open drawers and had no luck in finding the journal Allie gave Patrick the night before. She decided he may have left it somewhere and hadn't had time to write in it before his unfortunate death. She realized that the wedding celebration could have easily muffled unusual noises coming from the guest rooms. Mac told her Patrick drowned, but so far, no other information was ready from the coroner.

Brenda shuffled through an overnight bag and with a flood of relief she recognized the Sheffield Bed and Breakfast's logo on a small journal stashed underneath a sweater. She flipped it open. Patrick had written a short paragraph in it.

What a surprise. Not just Alexandra here, but others from my past. It leaves me almost speechless. It's a good thing I love the water since that's where I plan to spend most of my time while I'm here. I thought I would have much more privacy here, instead everything seems to have followed me. Much to my regret, I may have to check out sooner than I planned. Swam two miles today in under an hour, a personal record…

Brenda put the journal down, more interested in the revelation about Alexandra than about Patrick's swimming records. She tried to envision the timid Alexandra Cornell being involved in a drowning – not just any drowning, but one of a man who was obviously a strong swimmer. Alexandra was slender-framed, a meek woman, and had given no indication of knowing anyone when she checked in. Alexandra's lack of self-confidence was something else to consider; was it all a façade? It troubled Brenda to think that Patrick had recognized not only Alexandra but unnamed other people from his past. However, there were no more details, as he had only written one page in the journal.

"I know one thing for sure. Alexandra could never have transported a body in a large suitcase anywhere," Brenda muttered as a soft knock indicated the two plainclothes officers had arrived.

She slipped the journal into an evidence bag and told one of the officers to make note of the find and continue looking for anything else. Phyllis stood at the doorway and then excused herself. She had no intention of interfering in a crime scene and worriedly headed downstairs to make sure no one started asking questions about strangers poking around in a guest's room.

Brenda told the officers she wanted to take the journal with her and discuss it with Mac. Both men agreed. They sealed it up and logged the find and then handed it over. She hurried to the cottage and called Mac to explain the find and read Patrick's words to him.

Mac did not know what to make of it. "The only connection Alexandra may have is knowing he was here. We'll have to ask her to elaborate on their past. But I agree, there is no way she could have carried it out alone. She comes across as someone who is afraid of her own shadow," Mac mused. Brenda agreed with Mac.

That evening when guests appeared for dinner, Brenda noted Sandra and Shane glancing around.

"I haven't seen that fellow Patrick all day," Shane said.

"I'm beginning to miss his outspoken conversation style."
He chuckled. "I like it when people speak their minds. It's
refreshing these days."

Brenda smiled but did not reply. So far, none of her
guests appeared aware that Patrick wasn't going to come
to dinner again.

"He's probably either in a gym somewhere or running
along the beach," Rick said. "That seems to be his greatest
interest."

Alexandra kept her eyes downward. She picked at her
salad with her fork until finally nabbing a bite on the end
of the tines. It took a while for her to chew and swallow it
before deciding to take a second stab at it.

Brenda and Mac engaged guests in conversation. "Are
you enjoying the town, Daniel?" Brenda asked. She didn't
miss Alexandra's look. The young woman's eyes darted
over to drink in Daniel's words.

Daniel didn't look directly at Brenda as he spoke. He
took a drink of iced tea. "This is a beautiful town. I've
enjoyed the antique shop in particular. But Morning Sun
Coffee is the place to be. It's better than the news. All the
gossip passes through there."

"What's the latest?" Sandra asked.

"Shane mentioned Patrick, right? Well, I think he could
be the person everyone around Sweetfern Harbor is
talking about." Daniel looked uncomfortable when he
said it.

No one spoke until Brenda said, "What makes you
say that?"

Daniel shrugged. "Nothing in particular. I just picked
up that someone was dead and they're trying to find out

why or how. With Patrick not showing up, I just came to the inevitable conclusion. Maybe he's the one they're talking about."

"What about it, Detective Rivers?" Shane said, "Could he be right?" There were a few gasps, and everyone turned to look at Mac. Daniel cleared his throat uncomfortably, looking embarrassed.

Brenda and Mac glanced at each other. They did not know how many guests already knew that Mac was a detective, but now the secret was out.

"We don't know much at this point," Mac said. "But enough about work. Who's ready for dessert? I hear the new chef has baked up a fresh blueberry pie."

Brenda excused herself to fetch the dessert from the sideboard as the servers from the kitchen cleared everyone's dinner plates. In the bustle of the end of dinner, she did not miss that Alexandra and Daniel exchanged a strange glance, and Daniel's brow furrowed in anger before he left the table, leaving his pie untouched.

3

SUMMONS

Brenda and Mac decided to gather guests together the next morning before they scattered for the day. It was time to announce Patrick Anderson's untimely death. For now, all information regarding where he was found would be kept secret.

Several guests stopped to greet Allie in the front reception area before going into the dining room.

"We plan to head down to the beach first thing after breakfast. Jonathan Wright offered us a sailing trip out in the harbor this morning," Carrie said. "We decided to take him up on it." She latched onto Rick's arm. Allie smiled and told them to have a good time as they entered the dining room.

Once everyone had filled their plates from the buffet, Brenda and Mac joined them. They remained standing, and Mac called for attention.

"Since the news is beginning to get out, we wish to announce that an investigation is underway into the death of guest Patrick Anderson, who was found dead," Mac said with a steady and commanding voice. "We will be taking statements this morning and I encourage anyone with information to come forward immediately."

"So, he is the drowned person they found," Shane Dickinson said in a shocked whisper.

"But he knew how to swim," Alexandra blurted out. Everyone's head jerked in her direction. She fumbled with her hands and rested them in her lap. "I mean...he swam. In the ocean, I mean."

No one spoke at first. Alexandra began to tremble with nervousness at all the attention. Carrie patted her on the shoulder. "I know it's very upsetting, my dear, but these things happen. Even expert swimmers can have accidents. The sea is a dangerous place."

Brenda discreetly asked Phyllis to ensure the guests did not talk amongst each other too much in the dining room, then waited with Mac at the front desk for the guests to emerge from the dining room. Each one would give a statement. Rick Dawson smiled crookedly when Mac asked if they could speak in the nearby alcove.

"No pressure. It is just routine procedure," Mac said. They sat down on the two small wingback armchairs situated in the alcove by a small table. "When did you last see Patrick?"

Rick sat back in his chair for a moment. "I suppose that would be...before the wedding sometime. I headed out with Carrie. We didn't attend the wedding. I saw him around a couple times."

"Did you speak to him?" Mac asked. Rick indicated he

did not speak more than a few words. "What did you think of Patrick?"

A full-blown grimace filled Rick's face. "I won't lie. I didn't like the man at all. He was annoying, and his rudeness grated on me." He leaned back, long legs sprawled on the carpet between them. "Not the kind of man you make friends with, if you catch my drift." He leaned forward, elbows on his knees, thinking. "Shame he drowned. I saw him swimming down at the beach on my way down to the main street on my first day. He clearly knew what he was doing out on the water."

While he spoke, Mac glanced several times at Rick's hands and forearms. No scratches or marks of any kind were visible. The detective excused him and walked out with Rick. He motioned for Daniel Swift to join him.

Daniel seemed annoyed to have to even answer questions.

"Look, I'm sorry he's dead, but I don't know anything. I avoided him as much as possible," Daniel said. "He was obnoxious, to say the least. But surely you know that, you met him as a guest. I didn't see him after that first day, either. I drove out to a golf range up the highway, but it was closed, so I went to a sports bar for the night, hoping to wait out the wedding reception here at the bed and breakfast. I'm sorry, Detective, I wish I could tell you more. He was awful. Maybe Mr. Dickinson liked talking with people like that, but he turned me off almost instantly." The handsome car salesman seemed genuinely disturbed by the idea of someone so unlikeable, and Mac was favorably impressed by Daniel's attitude.

Mac had a few more minor questions and then told Daniel he could go about his day.

Brenda aimed for Alexandra Cornell. The woman's hands trembled ever so slightly, and Brenda noted moisture dotting her forehead. The sitting room was empty. They sat across from one another in the paisley Queen Anne chairs. Brenda opted to begin with social questions to try to put the obviously nervous woman at ease.

"I get the impression you know Daniel Swift. Are you two friends?"

Her eyes darted from side to side before settling on Brenda's face. "I knew him in college. We dated. We were very much in love. I have to say I was…happy to see him here this weekend. He's as handsome as ever."

"Have you stayed in touch since then?"

"I wish it were so, but…" Alexandra looked uncomfortable. "Not exactly."

Brenda took aim with a pointed jest: "Sounds like you still carry a torch for him," she teased. "Does your boyfriend know about him?"

"I don't have a – I'm single. I suppose you could say…I never fell out of love with Daniel. He's been married twice already, and both ended in divorce. I mean, so I've heard," the woman blushed. "It's a sign. He hasn't realized yet. I was the right one all along."

Brenda's adrenaline perked up. This was the most she had heard Alexandra say in one sitting. It was also the first time she saw a distinct physical beauty about the woman, now that she relaxed a little. Her body was taut and lithe when she sat straight in her chair without hunching over.

It was time to get serious. "What about Patrick Anderson? How did you know him?"

Alexandra looked down again and twisted her fingers again. "I don't. I mean, I didn't. I just watched him swimming a couple times. It was hard to take your eyes off him. He was an expert. I still don't see how he could have drowned. Do you think he got a cramp? Or maybe he got tangled in something?" Alexandra's eyes seemed desperate for answers.

"I can't share any details," Brenda said. "We're just trying to discover if there are any witnesses. When's the last time you saw him?"

"Not since before the wedding, obviously. He never came, and neither did Daniel." Alexandra sighed and then stood up quickly. "I want to get down to the shops if it's all right with you. I'm sorry I can't help. I certainly didn't see anything happen, if that's what you're trying to get at." She looked slightly angry now and Brenda moved to reassure her.

"No, Alexandra. We are asking everyone these same questions. Thank you for your time. Enjoy your day downtown."

Brenda told Mac she was going to walk into town to talk to Jonathan Wright. "He may have some information. He might be able to tell us more about Patrick Anderson's time on the water, what habits he had, if he mentioned any plans. Jonathan's always down at the beach or the docks."

"When he isn't hanging around Molly at the coffee shop," Mac commented and they both laughed. Jon's longstanding love for Molly was well-known as Jonathan often found excuses to head to Morning Sun Coffee for extended mid-morning breaks. Mac told her he would see her later.

Down at the harbor's edge, Brenda spotted Jonathan giving final instructions to a tourist. Brenda headed in his direction. She told him of the investigation into the drowning of Patrick Anderson. He stood with his hands on his hips, puzzled and sad.

"There is no way he drowned," Jon said. "Is Mac sure of that?"

"The coroner confirmed that was the cause of death. How strong of a swimmer would you say he was?"

"His skills went way beyond any kind of scale...I mean, he could be a lifeguard, that's how strong a swimmer he was. I saw him swim a mile out into the harbor. Where did it happen?"

"That's unknown right now. The body was not found on the beach, so we presume it was taken out of the water along the beach down here. Did you notice anyone hanging around, anything that was different when he was down here?"

"He came alone for the most part. Of course, most people on the beach couldn't take their eyes off him when he stripped off his shirt for a swim. You don't see people with that kind of physique every day. He's almost acrobatic, the way he liked to dive into the ocean from the docks. He knew everyone watched him and could put on quite a show. He wasn't as good at sailing as he was at swimming, but he was still pretty good at it." Jon laughed shortly. "I have to admit I was glad when he focused on swimming that day. He came by and was very critical of the way I handled my business. Twice I was sure he was going to run off a customer. He was so rude, judgmental. I guess that explains why he came down here alone."

"He didn't talk to anyone in particular?" Brenda asked.

"No one he was friendly with." Jon shook his head in disbelief. "Can you believe he insisted on giving me fitness advice? He said I was never going to be an elite sailboat racer or some such nonsense. He bragged about how most people go about building muscle all wrong. Listen to me... I guess I've complained enough about him. What a tragedy that he drowned."

"We need to hear everything. He mentioned he was going to eat a light lunch and head right down here," Brenda said. "Any information you have would be helpful."

Jon offered to provide receipts showing when the man had briefly rented a one-person sailboat to scope out the swimming conditions in the center of the harbor. Brenda asked him to drop off photocopies at the police station, then thanked him and left. She walked along the sand and breathed in the salt air. She had nothing concrete yet. It was time to think about Alexandra's words. The abrupt ending to their conversation raised a red flag, but it could simply be nervousness. Daniel Swift definitely avoided Alexandra as much as possible, which made Brenda all the more curious to hear his side of the failed romance between the two of them.

Brenda wished she could spend the rest of the day watching the seagulls and listening to the quiet lapping of waves. Her peaceful reverie was interrupted by a call from Mac.

"It's official, Brenda," he said. "The coroner confirmed

ocean water and sand was found in Patrick's lungs, consistent with a person being submerged and drowned in seawater. There are also minor injuries, likely from when he was put in the footlocker. However, the actual cause of death was strangulation, not drowning. We think the killer or killers thought he was dead and then realized he was still alive, so he was finished off by strangulation."

It was an ugly detail. Brenda shuddered. She looked around at the waves, which looked less peaceful now and more threatening. "I'm still at the beach. Do you want me to look around for evidence? Did the coroner give us a better idea of where this happened?"

"We're not sure which beach area to check, but you could rule things out by taking a look. My guys have already combed the dunes and beaches north of the main street, so maybe you can check the south areas. I hope the tide hasn't washed away any evidence. Call me if you see anything."

Brenda headed to the south portion of the beaches and watched children building sandcastles at the water's edge. Two young couples stretched out on beach towels. One father cautioned his children to stay away from the water until they could all enjoy it together. Brenda realized she was heading closer and closer to the part of the beach near the bed and breakfast. If she looked up past the seawall and the scrub bushes in the sand, she could see the roof of the bed and breakfast.

She walked to the point where the sand turned to pebbles and then rock. Taking out her phone, she snapped several photos of undisturbed sand and pebbles. Then, on closer scrutiny, she noted a deep, double imprint behind a log that had washed ashore. The imprints looked as if they had been left by something heavy dragged through the sand. She immediately called Mac, who in turn said he would send an officer down to meet her.

"What are the measurements of the trunk the body was in?" Brenda said, scanning the disturbed sand around her.

Mac gave her the dimensions. "Officer Thompson will measure what you've found. We may have our crime scene. Are there beachgoers down there now?"

Brenda told him of the two families and several others who were nearby. She did not tell Mac yet, but she was disturbed by the thought that this area of the beach was easily viewable from the side garden of Sheffield House. That was exactly where everyone had stood and celebrated her father's wedding just the other night. She waited impatiently for Officer Thompson to arrive. The deep imprint in the sand matched the dimensions of the footlocker. He snapped photos and then strung yellow tape around the area and called Mac while she listened in.

"Detective Rivers, I've taped off the section. We're starting to attract attention. Do you want me to stay down here?"

Mac told him yes and that he was on his way. The four adults on the towels now watched with fascination. None of them asked what was going on until Brenda walked past them on her way back to Jonathan's boat rental shed. She did not want to risk walking from the crime scene directly to her own home, thus drawing attention to the proximity of the two places.

"It is just something the police want to take a look at," she told the people watching. "There's no threat to anyone's safety. I'm sure it's nothing." She reassured them, pretending yellow crime scene tape on the beach was normal.

She met Mac back at the police station and told him of her fears. He reassured her that there was no way to know the connections between the crime scene and the bed and breakfast and emphasized that more detailed questioning would be necessary.

Brenda told him most of the guests were out for the day, but she would stay around the bed and breakfast and notify each person one by one. It was decided to begin formal questioning at three that afternoon.

When Brenda spoke with Allie about the newest developments, the young reservationist felt badly about her rude interaction with Patrick Anderson. Brenda reassured her that most received similar treatment from the man. "You're not alone, Allie. Try not to dwell on it. We still have guests to deal with. Speaking of…do you have a list of exactly which guests attended the wedding and the reception?"

"I don't have a list," Allie said, "but I do know who told me directly they didn't plan on going. They were all very nice about it. No one except the Dickinsons knew Tim and Morgan, so it was understandable." She told Brenda she was sure Carrie, Rick and Daniel had not attended. She had seen for herself the others were there for most of the celebrations. "I'm not sure who left when. I'm sure some folks went up to their rooms for a bit to get refreshed and then came back down for more dancing. We can't rule that out, I mean."

"What about Patrick? Did he say whether or not he planned to attend?"

Allie shook her head no. "I spoke with him when he signed in and once more when he was on his way to the beach. I didn't see him at all after that. He could have been at the wedding. I didn't see him there, but I wasn't paying attention." She paused. "Ask Phyllis about him. I saw her talk briefly with him that first day, maybe he told her something more about his plans."

Brenda knew she would see Phyllis later, so first she headed back to her cottage. Jenny had left her a note to tell her she was at her shop. Brenda called Mac and told him she was on her way to the police station to prepare for the questionings. None of the guests presented objections when she told them to come down as part of routine procedure.

At three sharp, Carrie Porter and Rick Dawson arrived. Carrie was escorted into one interrogation room and Rick into the second room to wait his turn. Carrie Porter sat down across from Mac. When she saw Brenda walk in and sit down next to her husband Mac, her mouth opened wide with surprise.

"Are you a police officer too, Brenda?"

"I am an investigator with the force when it's called for. Mainly, my job is to run Sheffield Bed and Breakfast." Brenda smiled reassuringly, and Mac assured Carrie that Brenda's role was official within the department. Carrie expressed admiration for such an accomplishment.

"What can you tell us about Patrick's death?" Brenda asked.

Carrie shrugged her shoulders. "I didn't know him,

and frankly, I didn't care to. He was pretentious and obnoxious, not friendly at all. I'm sorry he's dead, but I'm just speaking the plain truth. The man was rude."

"Thank you for being candid. I know you didn't attend the wedding. Where did you spend your time that evening?" Brenda held her eyes on the petite blonde across from her.

Carrie thought back. "I spent the entire time downtown. I window-shopped and purchased a few things. I have receipts to show you." When asked if she was alone, Carrie said, "I tried to reach Rick to get him to join me, but his phone was dead. He apologized later. He gets careless about keeping his cell charged. I doubt he checked it the night before and it died long before he realized it."

Brenda and Mac exchanged glances. "What time did you catch up with him?" Mac asked.

"We finally connected around seven or maybe a little later. I was back at the bed and breakfast by then and he came in. We went to the Italian restaurant to eat. The wedding reception was underway by then and it was quite some party." She turned to Brenda. "I know we could have enjoyed the Hawaiian buffet along with your guests, but we both love Italian and wanted a more intimate setting."

There wasn't much to glean from Carrie Porter. When Rick was asked how he spent his time when Carrie was trying to reach him, he produced his trademark grin. "I took a long walk along the shoreline. I enjoyed the time alone. I found out later Carrie was upset because I didn't answer her calls, but I guess my battery died. I can't keep track of that thing. I'd much rather enjoy the scenery. I'm not really a shopping kind of guy anyway."

"What kind of business are you in? Don't you need to keep it charged for work calls?" Brenda challenged him.

"I'm an anesthesiologist. We're actually required to keep our cell phones off when we're working. The hospital gives us these electronic badges that have a paging and calling function built right in, so we can always be reached when we're on duty. I work eight-hour shifts and sometimes more. I'm not that into electronics in my spare time, honestly. I can barely work that badge pager thing even though I've been in that job forever."

"Did you know Patrick Anderson?" Mac asked.

His face didn't change but he blinked with annoyance. "You asked me that before and I have the same answer. Do you want me to repeat it?"

Mac stared at him. "Please do."

Something in Rick's answer sounded belligerent to Brenda as he told them again. There was no new information forthcoming. Afterward, Mac advised Rick and Carrie to stick around town.

"Great. We don't have anywhere we plan to go," Rick said. He sauntered over to join Carrie.

Before they moved to the next person, Brenda discussed her take on Alexandra Cornell and the couple they just interrogated. "I don't have a good feeling about any of them. I can't pin anything down, but something just isn't right." Mac agreed.

"We have to keep digging, Brenda," he reminded her. "Someone knows something."

When she left the station, Brenda was ready to close

her car door when Sandra and Shane Dickinson pulled in next to her.

"Can we talk with you in private somewhere, Brenda?" Shane said out his window. He leaned across his wife, who had lowered her window. Surprised, Brenda told them to follow her to a nearby city park, not wanting to spook them by taking them to an interrogation room right away.

Several children in the distance climbed and swung around on the playground equipment while parents chatted with one another from the park benches. Brenda chose a table under the picnic pavilion, close to the parking lot. Sandra and Shane followed her, and they all sat down.

"Your father told us you once worked for a private detective when you were still living in Michigan," Sandra said hesitantly. "We don't want to gossip, but…we've noticed some things that have us wondering." Brenda encouraged her to continue. Sandra motioned for her husband to speak.

"At first I didn't think much of it. We came for your dad's wedding and to enjoy our time around Sweetfern Harbor. This may be nothing, but we feel we should mention it." Brenda grew concerned and told him to go on. "Just before the wedding started, we passed near Daniel Swift and Rick Dawson talking together in the downstairs hallway. Rick seemed to be bragging a little and…well, we heard him talking about how sometimes people died on the operating table because of miscalculated anesthesia. He insisted it wasn't his fault, but he had seen it happen. He said something like, you'll never believe who tried to frame me for it. And Daniel was very interested in hearing more."

"I told Shane they were probably just talking nonsense," Sandra said. "But later Rick came up to me and started a friendly conversation and it made me think. He said Patrick was a fool to go out swimming so late, he kept going on and on about how dangerous it was. He said even good swimmers sometimes have accidents and drown. Daniel was there too, and he seemed upset about the whole thing. But strangest of all was when I saw Daniel's eyes go dark with anger. I looked behind me to see what caused him to be so upset. It was Alexandra. You know, the shy woman? She was listening to our conversation from around the corner and Daniel must have seen her just then. If looks could kill..."

Sandra and Shane waited for Brenda's response. Brenda tried to fit this story in with everything she already knew about her guests and could not see the connections yet. "What you've told me could be very helpful."

"I think you should question Alexandra. She's certainly a champion eavesdropper, maybe she knows something." Sandra leaned back.

"I don't think we should try to tell Brenda her job, Sandra," Shane said.

Brenda smiled. "Actually, we'll take all the help we can get at this point. I suppose Alexandra could simply be a nosy person but it's worth digging deeper. A good investigator keeps all options open until the evidence points in the right direction."

"So, he was murdered for sure?" Sandra asked.

"There's no way it was just an accident?" She covered her mouth and shook her head sorrowfully.

"I wish I could give you a better answer, Mrs. Dickinson." Brenda felt certain everyone had heard the rumors about him being attacked in the water, but she was fairly certain no one yet knew about where his body had been taken after he died. "All we know is that his manner of death was drowning. Everything else is just questions."

The laughter of children playing in the park echoed around them and they walked back to their cars to head their separate ways.

4

OBSERVATIONS

Brenda drove back to Sheffield Bed and Breakfast and took a walk along the garden pathways. She spotted Rick on one of the benches that faced the budding mums. She took a seat at the opposite end of the bench, pretending to simply enjoy the view, and used the opportunity to ask about his job.

The medical field was one subject Rick Dawson seemed most caught up in. He told her the work could be tough, but he never regretted going into anesthesia.

"Do you, as a physician, have any experience with people drowning? Any idea how a good swimmer could drown?"

Rick shook his head. "I don't have a lot of experience in that area, but perhaps he was on a medication that interfered with his usual strengths and abilities. He could have been stung by a jellyfish. The ocean isn't safe for a solo swimmer. It can turn on you." He fixated on the mums. "Maybe he got caught on something in the water and couldn't get loose. Was he entangled in something?"

"No details are being released at this point, I'm afraid. I'm sure that will all be revealed soon enough."

The huge look of relief on Rick's face when Carrie interrupted them wasn't lost on Brenda.

"I thought you wanted to get into the water, Rick. Are you ready?"

Rick smiled at Carrie. "I'm ready. I was just waiting for you." They told Brenda they would see her at dinner that evening.

After the couple left, Brenda decided to take a walk along the shoreline. She heard more voices than usual down there and felt she could easily mix in unnoticed. At the top step before descending to the beach she watched Carrie and Rick observe the taped-off area on the beach. If they didn't already know, this surely told them where Patrick's death occurred. Did they also know he didn't end up there on the beach? She watched Carrie move her sandaled foot back and forth at the edge of the barrier. The officer on duty stepped forward and motioned to them to stay away since the area was off-limits.

The couple backed up a few steps and then stripped to their bathing suits and plunged into the water. Brenda watched while they stuck close together. Neither swam very far out and after ten minutes came out, dried off and slipped shorts and shirts over their wetsuits. While they readied themselves to leave, Brenda made her way back to the bed and breakfast unseen.

She called the coroner to ask what other evidence had been found in the body. He told her there was sand and seawater and nothing else, confirming that the deed began and ended on the beach. "Whoever did this likely had the footlocker down at the beach, in place." He hesitated. "For the life of me, I can't figure out how no one at all saw the crime in progress. It's still tourist season, and I'm surprised no one was on the beach. Mac and I have discussed this over and over with no idea of a lead. Of course, that's not my job…I expect the detective and you will figure this out. For now, I'm concentrating on the body."

"What was the time of death?"

"I have determined between six and eight o'clock."

Brenda was taken aback. "That was during the wedding. Most people were either at the reception or downtown to watch my father and Morgan in the limo parading by at that time. Jonathan Wright told me he closed early that night because of the celebration. He attended the wedding and so wasn't down at the water to witness anything. I wonder if any boats were passing by and saw anything?"

She called Mac and asked the same questions. "We've had three boaters come forward who were logged by the harbor or the docks as being along that beach area. None of them left from that beach or stopped there, though, and they saw nothing. So far, we can't be sure who else passed by but have put the word out that we're looking for witnesses."

"We should pay closer attention to our guests tonight. All of them will be here for dinner."

"I'll make sure I get there on time," Mac said.

Brenda hesitated. "Mac, I've been thinking. This has

everyone on edge. I wonder if your presence may make the guests hold back. Why don't you and William eat downtown? I'll ask Phyllis to join us. She's very good at noting quirks in people."

Mac laughed. "I get the point. You don't want interference. William and I could stand to have a good dinner together like the old times."

Detective Bryce Jones expected another long night at the police station. Jenny was happy to stay another night in the cottage where her dad and Brenda lived, just so she would not be alone. Brenda told her to have dinner with them. The expectant mother's appetite seemed endless. Jenny explained the baby must be a hungry one, but Phyllis always laughed and said she was going to serve her an extra heaping full plate that night, insisting her appetite was natural.

On her way to the table with Jenny, Brenda noticed Daniel standing outside the dining room door. Once inside, Brenda figured out why – Alexandra was in the dining room looking around at the guests. When she didn't see Daniel, she chose an empty chair at the end of the elongated oval table. Daniel entered after she sat down and chose a chair next to Jenny and far from Alexandra. Brenda saw Alexandra's disappointment that there were no empty chairs she could move to in order to get closer to him.

Rick and Carrie sat midway down the table. Neither spoke unless asked a question or someone made a comment to include them. Sandra and Shane carried on a conversation with Daniel and the other guests. No one brought up the subject of Patrick Anderson.

As guests moved toward the sitting room after dinner for desserts and drinks, Phyllis pulled Brenda aside. They agreed the only odd behavior noted was the subdued couple. Carrie and Rick opted to skip dessert and chose to take a walk downtown. Most shops remained open until nine during tourist season. Conferring, neither Brenda nor Phyllis knew whether to make anything of the couples' behavior and decided to watch the rest of the guests instead.

Daniel once again waited for Alexandra to settle in the corner of the room. He sat in one of the paisley armchairs furthest from her and talked briefly with Shane Dickinson. The conversations came to a halt when one guest asked how Patrick Anderson had died. When his name was spoken out loud, silence fell over the room.

Phyllis's eyes swept the room. Two seats away, Alexandra cowered back in her chair and glued her gaze on Daniel. Her face was ashen.

"Are you all right, Alexandra?" Phyllis asked. The woman nodded yes.

"How terrible to gossip about such things." Alexandra's voice was barely audible.

The guest apologized quickly and changed the subject. The conversation moved on, but Daniel did not. He gave Alexandra a glare and left the room. In the hubbub of conversation and the entrance of one of the servers with a fresh tray of desserts, Alexandra left without anyone noticing.

A lull finally ensued, and Brenda mentioned shops were still open downtown. Several guests took her up on her suggestion.

"When you have time, Brenda, we'd love a tour of the whole beautiful bed and breakfast," Sandra said.

"There's time right now. Anyone who wants a tour, follow me." Brenda managed to snag most of the remaining guests. All were eager to hear details about the restored Queen Anne structure. Brenda told them about the restoration process her uncle undertook.

"Are there any secret passageways?" Sandra asked.

"If there are, Randolph didn't leave me any hints. I suppose if they are secret, he hoped I'd find them one day on my own." The guests joked about hidden skeletons and secret passages. "There is a back stairway to the tower. Nothing has been done up there except work to preserve it. A new roof and sealing of windows were top priority for Randolph. I'll take you up there. Those stairs bypass the access to the attic. The tower is the smallest room in the bed and breakfast." She explained there was nothing to see but the view from the top, so she would proceed only if everyone was interested. Everyone was eager to do so.

The room was as cramped and odd as Brenda remembered it, and the guests crowded over to the narrow windows to look down at the lawn from the high vantage point and see the sea so far below. Above all, she wished she could get a viewpoint like this one on the current case. It seemed everywhere they turned there was a new dead end.

When they went back downstairs, Phyllis told Brenda who had left the bed and breakfast to pursue their own interests. Everyone dispersed, and Brenda sat down in the sitting room with Phyllis. They determined Brenda should try to talk casually with Alexandra again. Brenda felt Alexandra might have gained more confidence since no startling developments had come forth. The guest obviously held secrets of her own, and Brenda was adamant to get to the bottom of the reason for her strangely timid nature and, above all, her odd interactions and history with Daniel.

A few minutes later, Brenda put on her best smile and found Alexandra reading a book at the end of the porch and asked if she enjoyed the night air. Alexandra told her yes. Brenda casually leaned against the railing to gaze at the gardens below.

"I heard you say you moved around often as a child. Did you ever live in New England?"

"No, sadly," Alexandra said, looking out at the beautiful evening too. "It's so lovely here."

"All that moving...a military family, I'm guessing?"

"How did you know? My father was an army man. We moved like clockwork." She laughed softly but with little mirth. "I guess it's in my blood now. I still haven't put down roots. I have no trouble finding secretarial jobs, but they grow boring and I move on." She shook her head. "I'm sure that's boring to you too, Brenda, I'm sorry." Before Brenda could protest, Alexandra continued awkwardly, "No, it's fine. I know why I don't have close friends. They all get tired of me pining after Daniel. Logic tells me to forget him, but my heart tells me I shouldn't give up hope. I have a good chance. Especially when I heard of his second divorce..."

Brenda could not afford to lose Alexandra's confidence now and decided to take these quixotic romantic inclinations at face value. Perhaps she wasn't a stalker after all. "If I were you, I would just enjoy life. Let him – or anybody, really…friends, boyfriends – see you doing things you really enjoy. Then what you want, or who you want, will just come naturally. Often, it's a matter of relaxing and letting things flow."

"That's an interesting way to look at life. I've never been good at…relaxing."

At this point, Brenda leaned in with concern on her face. "I noticed you were tense earlier, too…you found it hard to listen to talk of Patrick's death, didn't you? Poor thing…"

The old Alexandra returned. Her face grew pale and she shrank back. "I don't like to talk about death."

"Even if you know something that could help us?"

Alexandra looked away, fidgeting with the corner of her book. "I don't know what you mean."

Brenda pressed her, and Alexandra's eyes darted around the porch in the near-darkness and she looked lost. "I don't know for sure and for that reason I don't want to start more rumors. Goodnight, Mrs. Rivers." She snapped her book shut, then darted into the house and strode up the winding staircase to her room.

Brenda didn't know if she should look at their conversation as a victory or if the road to reaching the truth with Alexandra had just grown bumpier. She asked Phyllis to join her on the veranda. They watched guests returning to the bed and breakfast. Carrie and Rick came from the beach, accompanied by Daniel Swift. They chatted with Brenda and Phyllis briefly and went inside.

"I've noticed Carrie and Rick aren't around much at all," Brenda said. Phyllis agreed. "They seem to be at the beach almost all day." Phyllis guessed they were probably just the outdoors type, and Brenda agreed.

The next morning, Allie told Brenda she had been thinking about who brought in the larger suitcases. Brenda had sworn her to secrecy when she told her receptionist the full story of Patrick's death.

"Daniel carried too much luggage in. One suitcase was huge. Carrie and Rick also came in with enough luggage to stay two weeks rather than the four days they booked."

"You are right about the large suitcases you saw, but we're trying to track down something a lot larger, like a footlocker size."

Allie was about to ask more questions, but then Brenda's cell rang. Brenda walked down the hall to the library room and closed the door behind her for privacy. Mac told her they had results of fingerprints on the footlocker. Many were found, which indicated it had likely been through more than one owner.

"It could have been in someone's basement for years. Or bought secondhand, picked up at the dump, something like that," Mac said, explaining their next avenue of exploration.

"I don't think you'll find the extra fingerprints belong to anyone related to the case we've questioned so far," Brenda said.

"I agree. We'll have to eliminate them, though."

Brenda thought again about Allie's mention of the guests who had lugged in large suitcases. One in particular she described could have been a footlocker. On the other hand, Brenda thought, who would use a footlocker as a suitcase? Surely Allie was mistaken. According to her reservationist, Rick Dawson carried the largest luggage, and Allie thought for sure a body could have fit into it. In the end, Brenda felt she was belaboring that point more than necessary. She had later seen the case Patrick was stuffed into and it wasn't a suitcase. She knew if they could track down the source of the fatal footlocker, they could then trace it to the buyer.

Most of the guests had booked extended stays in Sweetfern Harbor before arriving. However, the events since their arrival seemed to have changed everyone. Alexandra, predictably, began spending more time in her room. Carrie and Rick barely spoke during mealtimes and were never around. Daniel Swift scowled at Alexandra when their eyes met. Finally, after one meal, he waited for Alexandra outside the dining room. Brenda didn't miss the way Alexandra's eyes lit up when Daniel told her he wanted to talk with her. Brenda slipped unseen into the passageway alcove. She closed the door but left a narrow opening, so she could hear the conversation.

"Daniel…it's so good to finally talk. All this time I thought you were trying to avoid me. I told myself that was just my imagination."

"You're not imagining things, Alexandra. I am avoiding you, but it seems you are bent on annoying me at every turn. If you continue to act like this, I will not tolerate it. You will not like it if that happens."

Brenda heard the gasp echo in the hall. "I promise I

won't say a thing about what happened, Daniel. I'll leave you alone if that's what you really want."

"What's that supposed to mean?"

Alexandra stammered. "No…nothing at all. I don't know why I said it like that. I meant…I promise I won't follow you around any longer."

Silence followed her comment. Brenda knew they both stood there and could only imagine the fear and timidity on Alexandra's face and sheer anger on Daniel's. She could almost feel the tension between them. She heard Daniel's heavy footsteps finally retreat. When she exited the alcove and walked down the hallway, the expression on Alexandra's face sent Brenda's mind into a whirlwind. She saw a mixture of vulnerability and even madness in the woman. Brenda hesitated and then Alexandra met her eyes. Once again, her eyes held timidity along with fear.

"Are you all right? I think you should have a hot cup of tea, Alexandra. Try to get some rest. I don't know what has upset you, but try and relax."

Alexandra seemed to cling to the proffered empathy. She nodded her head in agreement. In Brenda's mind, there was no time to waste, though she knew she must proceed cautiously with the fragile woman. She brought two cups of lemon verbena tea into the sitting room and closed the doors.

"Tell me why you are so upset, Alexandra."

The teacup rattled when her guest placed it on the saucer. She shook her head adamantly. "I promised. If I don't keep my promise, I don't know what he may do…"

Brenda opted to take this drama with a grain of salt. "I doubt anyone would want to harm you, Alexandra. Who did you make this promise to? Did they threaten you? Does someone want to hurt you?"

Alexandra looked shaken. "Daniel clearly isn't going to realize he loves me. My whole vacation here has been fruitless."

"Sometimes we can love with all our heart and the person we love doesn't reciprocate. That's not so unusual, though it can hurt deeply."

Alexandra sipped the tea. This time the rattle of the cup onto the saucer settled and she seemed to calm herself. "I thought all these years I could convince him to marry me." Her eyes hardened with no warning. "He just doesn't get it. Men can't see when the right woman is right in front of them."

Brenda suddenly wished she hadn't come in alone with the woman. She had plenty to say to her, but the fiery look in Alexandra's eyes told Brenda that the scorned woman wasn't on the same plane as anyone else in the matter.

"Perhaps I should have brought you some chamomile tea…you look tired, I think. Have you been sleeping well at night?"

Alexandra returned to her shy demeanor. "I've never been one to sleep through the night. I often wake up from nightmares." She smiled at Brenda. "Don't worry about me, Brenda. I spend most of my time alone except when I'm at work. It gives me too much time to think."

There was no doubt in Brenda's mind that she had to talk with Mac right away. Before she and Alexandra left the room, Brenda noted her guest's hands wrapped around the teacup. Her slender fingers made Brenda think of an elegant piano player. Her skin stretched over the delicate knuckles looked fragile, but perhaps there was a hidden strength there.

Once she had returned to their cottage and settled herself on the loveseat, Brenda called Mac.

"There is something seriously wrong with Alexandra Cornell," she said. "I think she either has vital information about Patrick's murder, or she needs mental health therapy. Or both." She told Mac about the whole encounter. "For a moment, she really scared me. Her eyes changed from normal, shy maybe, to something more than anger. It was more than manic. It was like insanity. I'm certain she knows more, Mac. But every time I push, she retreats into her shyness and claims to know nothing."

"We should bring her down here as soon as possible. I'll have Officer Thompson join us. He's a trained psychologist as well as an excellent officer of the law."

Brenda agreed with the plan. Then she was left with the dilemma of figuring out how to invite Alexandra down to the police station for a follow-up interrogation without upsetting the woman's delicate mental balance.

5

WITNESSES

Alexandra Cornell stretched out on the luxurious bed. She knew she wouldn't sleep, but she had time to think while alone. She spent a lot of time alone, and a lot of time thinking. She had been alone, it seemed, since her childhood.

She had been only three or four years old when she realized that watching her parents pack up all the household belongings was something to expect with upsetting regularity. Every year, it seemed, out came the boxes, in drove the moving truck, away went her toys and her clothes and everything familiar, and she was driven to another sad, empty, blank slate of a house, and dumped in a school where she knew no one and no one wished to know her.

By age six, she dreaded it and began to have nightmares regularly. She complained to her mother and father that she didn't want to move again. That time, they were going to live in Japan. At the time, all she knew was that she was supposed to be excited to be going all the way across the ocean. She pictured crossing high over the deep blue sea, which reached up to pull her down in her dreams every night.

Alexandra, you're such a lucky little girl, her father had told her. *No more crying about the move, you'll upset your baby brother,* her mother had scolded, sheltering two-year-old Oliver in a protective embrace.

Her father had been right on some counts. Alexandra eventually became mesmerized with the art and culture of the Japanese people and their country. Her family lived there for four years and on the military base she befriended other children from various backgrounds and countries, happily forgetting her troubles. Until she noticed the cardboard boxes begin to appear again. She threw a temper tantrum so loud the neighbors heard it through the walls. Her father was at work and her mother had no patience for the ten-year-old's moods, no matter how fearsome. To this day, Alexandra realized she never understood how hard it had been on her mother.

When Alexandra was finally old enough to be allowed to stay in the United States alone and then attend college on the East Coast, she was ready to enjoy living in one place for four whole years. The day arrived in the middle of her first semester when it hit her that once she graduated, she could choose her own life. Yet she had no idea where she would go.

Then she met Daniel Swift. Their attraction was quick, perhaps because she was so overwhelmed with attraction that she practically threw herself at him. When he mentioned he planned to return to his small hometown and start his own business after graduation, this drew her even closer. She imagined a perfect small-town life, raising a family with Daniel in a house where her own children would never have to face the terror of constant moves. Not if she had anything to say about the matter.

Only a month after she began dating Daniel, Alexandra received terrible news. It was the darkest day of her young life. Her mother, deep in an untreated depression, had poisoned Alexandra's teenaged brother Oliver, and then committed suicide. The family lived so far away that Alexandra could not even travel to join her father for the funerals.

Her father distanced himself emotionally from Alexandra after that, though he continued to pay her tuition. The horrific deaths unraveled the young woman. Caught between her perfect dream of a future with Daniel and the ghastly nightmare of grief for her mother and brother, she failed to move forward at all.

Daniel noticed her erratic behavior and tried to help, but she resisted fiercely. Fights quickly damaged the relationship past the point of repair. He understood her grief, but he was not willing to be dragged down into her paralysis. He broke off all contact with her. When Alexandra would not let him go so easily, he transferred to a different college in West Virginia. After their time together, Daniel proved how driven he was when it came to his studies. For the most part, he aced his exams and moved forward.

Alexandra, however, barely made it to graduation day. Then she drifted from one job to the next and from one location to the next, spending most of her free time tracking Daniel's movements online or in person, driving slowly down the streets where he lived, or following his girlfriends or wives (or ex-wives), dissecting her brief relationship with him in her mind until she was torn apart with grief for the life they couldn't have together.

Her thoughts returned to the present. She watched the sun move higher into the sky through the high window in her room in the bed and breakfast. There was only one thing that would fix her solitude, she knew. There was only one future she wanted. If only she could reach it.

Alexandra shifted onto her side. Finally, she fell into a fitful sleep.

When she awakened, Alexandra knew she had merely added to the catalogue of nightmares she had been experiencing nightly since arriving at Sheffield Bed and Breakfast. The high wall, and the terrible depths of the blue ocean below. She suddenly laughed as a child would at a joke, then flinched and grew silent, eyeing the door to the hall and contemplating her next steps.

Brenda Sheffield Rivers sat in front of her laptop in the small office behind the reception desk. She read everything she could find about Alexandra Cornell and it turned out to be one eye-opener after another. No wonder Daniel stayed away from her. Alexandra needed counseling and had never received it, Brenda came to believe, judging from the unhinged letters to the editor the poor girl had published in town newspapers (a complaint about town statutes against stalking and loitering; a letter explaining why she was against mental health therapy for reasons of "independence and privacy") or police blotter entries for her minor infractions (ticketed for driving with no lights after dark on a residential road).

The record of Alexandra's obsessions read clearly on the screen. Brenda felt certain that whatever she knew about Patrick Anderson's death may very well be putting her over the edge. She could very well know something that could crack the case wide open.

Phyllis came from the kitchen after depositing odds and ends of dishes scattered in the sitting room. Brenda suggested they take a walk downtown before dinnertime. On the way, she told her friend about the conversation the evening before between Alexandra and Daniel.

"Do you really think she knows who killed Patrick?" Phyllis asked.

"I'm sure of it. I'm not so sure Daniel Swift is so innocent, either." The women discussed the strange relationship between the two. "She was terrified. I feel sure she has something to hang over his head, but on the other hand, she also comes across as a little crazy. It could all be chalked up to untreated mental illness, though. I can understand why Daniel doesn't want anything to do with her."

"He seems to be a friendly person," Phyllis said. "I can't imagine it's been easy on him. Even the kindest person in the world would get terribly exasperated being followed by a strange person like her all the time, don't you think? Anyway, I wonder if he and Alexandra knew Patrick. Aren't they all about the same age? Maybe they were in college together. And what about Carrie Porter and Rick Dawson? They've been so subdued since the murder. Not a word at dinners."

"You are right on all counts, Phyllis. There is a lot we haven't gotten out of any of them. Let's see what the gossip is at Morning Sun Coffee."

Only a few tables remained vacant and after ordering coffee, the women chose a cozy table near the entrance. Brenda waved at Carrie and Rick who sat in the far corner. Rick faced the wave and returned one. His smile appeared genuine. The couple bent their heads closer and seemed to return to a deep conversation.

"I wonder if those two attended the same college as Daniel and Alexandra." Brenda wondered a lot of things. Once she and Phyllis listened to talk in the coffee shop, she may have more to put together.

"That beach area is so nice and relaxing," a woman said. "I'm not so sure I want to go back down there where a drowning happened."

The man laughed. "It is roped off down the shoreline a distance. You wouldn't want to lounge around on pebbles and rocks anyway, Marcia. As for swimming in the Atlantic, that's why we're here. If you don't look at the roped-off area you wouldn't even know anything happened there."

The woman called Marcia shuddered. "I say we go to the next town up the coast and finish our weekend there." The man told her if that would ensure she enjoy their getaway, then they would do that.

An older man heard the conversation. "Don't believe the rumors. I heard he was murdered." Marcia gasped. He nodded his head smugly. "That's the rumor. He didn't just accidentally drown."

"How did he know that?" Phyllis whispered to Brenda. "I thought that was under wraps."

"It's supposed to be, but Sweetfern Harbor is such a small town. I suspect one of the guests said something and now it will become widespread. Let's get to the police station."

Phyllis Pendleton loved being in on crimes Brenda and Mac investigated. She knew to stand back when out of her league but enjoyed being allowed to stand close enough to help Brenda. She told her daughter Molly they were leaving. Molly was busy taking an order and told Phyllis she would see her later that evening. Molly and Jonathan were invited for dinner that night at the Pendleton house.

Chief Bob Ingram greeted Brenda and Phyllis when they came into the waiting room of the police station. A young woman sat with a tear-streaked face and a toddler clinging to her knee. The woman's face was bruised, and deep scratch marks were on her arms and beneath her right eye. The chief was telling her they were keeping her husband overnight and the judge would decide if he needed to be charged in the morning.

"I need him at home. I hope he won't be here long."

"You are lucky your neighbor called us. If he hadn't, you and your child would be dead by now. Officer Natalie Sims will take you to a shelter after you pick up a few belongings at your home. She will go in with you."

The chief turned on his heels without waiting to hear her protest. Brenda started to follow him to Mac's office.

"Is it all right for Phyllis to come in with us?"

"Sure, come on in, Phyllis. I hear you are a good observer. Maybe you can tell us a different side to this crime."

No one had to remind Phyllis about confidentiality. Brenda told Mac and Bob about the rumors floating around that Patrick's death was no accident. The chief told her he was not surprised it had leaked out.

"It may be a good thing. A witness we don't know about may come forward now that the word is out."

They all sat down. Brenda told him about the encounter between Daniel Swift and Alexandra Cornell. Chief Ingram listened intently. He agreed with the others that the guest may have vital information about the crime.

"She was at the wedding and the reception afterwards," Brenda said. "None of us paid attention to who came and went, it was so busy. She may have left for a while, or even been down at the beach. I feel sure she had nothing to do with the murder itself – her hands are so weak, and she's practically afraid of her own shadow. I really believe she is our key witness."

"Then get her down here," the chief said. Brenda explained Alexandra's fragile emotional state.

"I think I can talk her into coming on her own. Let me try that first. If that doesn't work, then we could have her arrested and forced to come down." She looked at Mac for his opinion.

"Perhaps an arrest will make her realize how serious a dilemma this is," he said. "It could prompt her to tell us everything just to make sure we leave her alone."

Brenda argued her point and they agreed to let her try it her way. Phyllis and Brenda left for Sheffield Bed and

Breakfast. The sooner Alexandra cooperated, the sooner Brenda could relax. She wondered about a lawyer for the woman, but that would be something to ask her after a possible arrest. Brenda crossed her fingers that the woman would not demand a lawyer as soon as she heard the police wished to question her further.

Alexandra was coming down the stairs when Brenda and Phyllis came through the front entrance. She looked ethereal on the stately stairs in a long skirt and wraparound sweater, and her smile was faint when she saw them. They watched as she gracefully descended the stairs.

Brenda asked her if she planned to go out for a while.

"I thought a little fresh air would be good. I think I'll take a walk downtown."

"Do you want some company?" Brenda asked.

"I'd love that. I've done a lot of thinking and my head feels like it's ready to burst wide open." The fleeting shadow of desperation crossed her expression before her amiable countenance returned.

"I'd like to take a walk downtown, too," Phyllis said. Even though they had just come from downtown, she had no intentions of leaving Brenda alone with Alexandra. Something about the guest caused the head housekeeper to shiver. Alexandra merely smiled and invited her along.

While Phyllis kept a conversation going about the signs of changing seasons about town, Brenda tried to think of the best way to convince Alexandra to keep going until they reached the police station. There were no cute shops next door to the police station or any convenient excuse to get her to walk down that street. But just then, Alexandra turned to Brenda.

"Where does your husband work?" This surprised Brenda. Everyone was well aware by now that Mac was a detective with the local police department. Alexandra had already had one interview.

"He's a detective, so he has an office at the police station, of course," Brenda said. She pointed ahead. "It's the building with the black roof down the hill a ways from here."

"I want to talk to him. Will he be there, or is he out solving crimes somewhere?" Alexandra's sharp laugh startled Brenda and Phyllis.

"He's probably there now. He spends this time of the afternoon reviewing evidence and interviewing people. His job is varied. Shall we drop in on him to say hello?"

Alexandra gave her a sidelong glance and jauntily stepped forward. The thirty-eight-year-old walked so quickly it was as if she was ready to start skipping. There was no doubt in Brenda's mind that the poor woman was on the brink of a complete mental collapse. Without further words, Brenda and Phyllis hurried to keep up with her manic pace.

Mac came from his office just as they entered the building. He glanced from Alexandra to Brenda and back. Brenda gave him a warning look. He took it in stride and welcomed Alexandra into his office, half giving her a tour and half soothing her with boring chatter. "I'm sure you just want to check in about your statement. I know it's a chore, so thanks for coming down."

Brenda told Phyllis to find the chief. Once Bob arrived

in the hallway, Phyllis waited anxiously in the front reception room to hear how it all played out.

"Shoot. I forgot that I have an evidence table set up in my office right now. Sorry, guess my office is off limits," Mac said with a shrug. "No guests allowed."

Brenda quickly understood what Mac was trying to do. "Let's head for one of those big empty rooms down the hall," she said, not alerting Alexandra to the fact that those rooms were in fact interrogation rooms, complete with recording equipment and one-way windows.

Alexandra told Mac she had plenty to tell him. He asked in a casual tone if she wanted a lawyer present. She waved her hand. "I don't need a lawyer. What I have to tell you is the truth." She jerked forward in her chair eagerly, like a child going for a lollipop.

"Do you mind if one of our officers comes in to listen as well?" Mac asked.

Alexandra's answer was again like someone much younger. "The more the merrier," she trilled with another laugh that abruptly trailed off.

Mac signaled for Officer Thompson to be called in. When he arrived, he greeted Alexandra warmly. Mac had previously told the psychologist about the woman and he was ready to assess her.

"Did someone tell you about your rights in here?" Officer Thompson asked Alexandra.

She shook her head. "Why do you keep asking that? Am I under arrest?"

"No, no," Mac reassured her. "It's just a formality. Do you wish to have a lawyer present?"

She hesitated and then asked, "Do I need one?" The recorder was on.

"Your choice. If it makes you feel more comfortable, you are allowed one with you."

Alexandra thought for a split second and then shook her head no again, her eyes lit from inside with a pale fury. "I don't need a lawyer telling what I can and can't say. I know things about certain people that others don't have a clue about. Some people pretend to be who they aren't, if you know what I mean."

Officer Thompson agreed with her. "I've met people like that but sooner or later those around them learn the truth about them."

"That's for sure."

A brief silence followed. Alexandra's face fell. The light that had been emanating from her face a few seconds before diminished. She seemed to curl into a knot.

"It's all right, Alexandra. I know you are afraid of something," Brenda said, "but you are protected here."

She uncurled her tense body only a fraction. "Protection? I've never trusted it in my life. My father never protected any of us. Did you know my mother killed my brother and then herself? My father didn't step in to protect Oliver, did he? I can see how he might not care about my mother. She didn't like him moving us around all the time any more than I did. She even told me once that she never wanted children. Can you imagine hearing that from your own mother?"

"No," Brenda said. "It must have been very hard on you. How old were you when this happened?"

"It was when I was in college. When I fell in love with

Daniel. I called and told her…and she said she never wanted children. Said I was ungrateful, abandoning the family…Daniel didn't like me getting so upset about it. That's partly why I still love him! He tried to shelter me in his own way…but he can be as mean as my father was."

"Sounds like you have a lot of pain in your life. Perhaps you've seen others in pain and wanted to help them. Is there something you've seen? Something you want to tell us?" Officer Thompson asked in a gentle but probing voice. "Do you have something to say about the death of that man found recently?"

A harsh laugh escaped Alexandra's mouth. "He didn't drown like all of you think. I watched him swim. I couldn't take my eyes off him. I kept thinking, those waves will take him down, but they never did. I thought maybe the ocean would get the revenge I never did…he was the one who broke up Daniel and me, you know." Officer Thompson asked how he caused the breakup. "He argued with Daniel about something. He was always after Daniel about something. I think Patrick hoped to date me when Daniel dumped me…maybe he was hoping I would be too sad to notice his slimy moves."

"You are telling us that Patrick was in college with you and Daniel?" Brenda asked. Alexandra nodded her head yes. "Who else knew Patrick?"

"I suppose lots of people."

"Think about the people who are staying at Sheffield Bed and Breakfast," Brenda said. "Did anyone else there know him?"

"I know Daniel did, and I did. I may have…fudged the truth when you asked me at first, but I did know him. He was so intolerable. I didn't want to admit I knew him." She laughed again. "I went to the gym daily but not because Patrick egged me to do that. I would never have done anything if asked by Patrick. I did it because I wanted to look my best for Daniel. But Daniel and me? We hated Patrick. We talked about how annoying he was many times, back in those days…"

Brenda had no intention of allowing her to drift off to the subject of Daniel again. "What did you see happen to Patrick, Alexandra?" Brenda said.

"Nothing," she said. "I only saw the ocean." Her tone was light, as if joking. Then she tensed up. "I can't be certain. What if I'm wrong? If I tell you anything, my life will be on the line. I'm not ready to die. Not before Daniel realizes we need to get back together…"

Mac knew if they arrested Alexandra Cornell, they would never get a full confession of what she saw. One night in a cramped jail cell could put her over the edge and send her straight to a mental institution. No amount of encouragement budged her to say more.

After she left, Brenda spoke. "I think she needs a thorough psych evaluation. We all know that if she voluntarily tells us what she witnessed, that will be the first order of business for any lawyer in her defense."

"That's true, if she indeed knows anything," Mac said. "Maybe she knows nothing about the crime at all. She's just playing games. Maybe she didn't see anything and just likes the attention."

Officer Thompson agreed she wasn't exactly a reliable witness at this point.

Phyllis looked up expectantly at Brenda when she

came walking out into the waiting area, and Brenda shook her head to indicate they had nothing. When they got outside, they saw Alexandra a block ahead of them. Her head was downcast, her demeanor reverted to the shyness and skittish fear she came in with the day of her arrival.

Brenda explained what had happened. "I think she'll have to be arrested to get the truth of what she may or may not know." She told Phyllis their options and possible outcomes.

"How to find out if she knows anything or not will be a serious dilemma," Phyllis agreed.

"The guys at the station think she may not know anything, but I have a strong feeling she does. She is so erratic, and that tells me she is trying to recover from what she saw." Brenda told Phyllis about Alexandra's comment about working out. "If she does go to the gym regularly, she doesn't look like it."

"Some people manage gym workouts and still keep slim and fragile-looking. It's something to think about." Phyllis paused. "She may not be as fragile as we think."

The women returned to Sheffield Bed and Breakfast without talking more about it. When they went inside, Brenda asked Allie if Alexandra had come in.

Allie pointed in the direction of the oceanfront. "She headed down that way and I haven't seen her come back." They all looked out the front windows of the Queen Anne mansion, and across the wide, manicured lawns the blue of the ocean turned gray as scudding clouds began to cover over the sunny afternoon skies.

6

MAIN SUSPECT

Brenda made a split-second decision and headed out across the lawns. Phyllis followed Brenda to the seawall, too. Alexandra walked precariously across the narrow part of the stone barrier. Her arms swung wildly as her balance teetered for a moment, and she sang a strange foreign tune.

Brenda recognized the melody vaguely and searched her memory before remembering it as a Japanese song, *Tanabata-sama*, one she had learned as a child. Her parents had taken her to a children's theatre in Michigan one year when a troupe visited from Japan and Brenda fell in love with that song. Her father later found the sheet music for it so her mother could teach her to play it on the piano.

"I know that song. It's 'Bamboo Leaves are Rustling.' She's singing in Japanese." Phyllis stared at her in surprise but decided to wait and ask Brenda later how she knew that. "We can't startle her. Let's wait here for her to get off the wall. If we shock her and she falls, she'll hurt herself on the slope. There's nothing but sharp rocks on the other side."

Alexandra tried to turn around and then tottered. Brenda and Phyllis held their breath until she hopped off toward the grassy side, onto Sheffield Bed and Breakfast's lawn. Looking frail and confused, she sat in a tangle of limbs on the soft grass. They hurried to ask her if she was all right.

"I'm just a little dizzy...I don't know what happened. I like to sit on the wall and watch the seagulls and boats. I must have tripped on something."

Alexandra looked surprised to find herself on the ground, yet her eyes appeared clear and calm. Brenda decided now was the time to ask questions while the ocean had calmed her emotions. "Is this where you were when you saw it?" Brenda ventured in a soft voice.

Alexandra gazed at the water and said without turning to the women, "I did see Patrick die out there. He was... held under the water. It was no accidental drowning. But you should talk to the killer, not to me."

Alexandra said no more and walked to her favorite, safer spot on the wall. She drew her knees up and rested her chin on them. While her body appeared calm, her eyes appeared distant now and almost glassy, as if in shock at having revealed so much.

Brenda and Phyllis went back to the bed and breakfast. Brenda called Mac. He sent two female officers to talk with Alexandra. When they arrived, she clammed up. Finally, she insisted that Daniel should be questioned again and refused to say anything further. Brenda conferred with the officers and together they had no idea if Alexandra was making up the accusation or not. Mac decided it was worth calling Daniel back in.

"Let me know how it goes, Mac. I must get back to work. I haven't checked on our guests all day." Mac told her he would tell her everything as soon as he had information.

Alexandra breathed the salt air with deep sighs. If she could live near the water for the rest of her life, she felt she may finally find peace. For the first time, she could rest her eyes on the exact spot where Patrick Anderson took his last breath. She felt calm now that she had said a little to the police. Patrick almost won midway through the battle for his life but in the end, he lost. The big black box was waiting at the edge of the water, the flat dolly next to it. Alexandra was terrified to reveal, however, that she knew exactly who brought it down there and who readied it for Patrick's body.

In the background of that horrible moment, watching the man's death under the saltwater waves, strains of the ukulele played a celebratory song. The wedding celebrants laughed and enjoyed life while Patrick worked his entire body and spirit to escape his fate, all to no avail.

Alexandra didn't feel remorse the man was dead. She understood why he was sought out and killed. It was the contrast between death on one side of the wall and life on the other that caught her attention. It was everything in the deep ocean that scared her.

She had every intention of keeping her knowledge a secret. That was her plan. It was the only thing that would unite her and Daniel, their shared knowledge. But then Daniel showed his true colors by rejecting her again. He

was the one who had to pay now and at last she would get
her revenge. Tears slipped down her face when she
thought about Daniel locked up in a prison cell
somewhere out of her reach. She vowed to make sure he
spent enough time there to miss her and then she would
tell the police she made it all up.

Daniel was playing pool in the guest recreation room
on the lower level of the bed and breakfast. He and Shane
Dickinson contested for top scores, and Daniel was ahead
for the moment. Both men held their cue sticks frozen in
their hands when two uniformed officers interrupted
the game.

"Daniel Swift?" one of them said. Daniel identified
himself, confused. "You are under arrest for the murder of
Patrick Anderson." He snapped handcuffs on the suspect
and read him his rights.

Daniel's face paled and switched to one of defeat. "I
want a lawyer."

"You can make the call when you arrive at the police
station."

Shane leaned forward and rested his hands on the cue
stick, in shock at what he was witnessing. He hoped the
police had the wrong person. He couldn't imagine the
amiable car dealership owner had any inclination to
murder. He swiftly left the recreation room to find
his wife.

"Brenda and Mac know what they're doing, Shane. I'm
glad they have a suspect finally. I was beginning to think
anyone here could have killed Patrick."

They discussed the subject for a few minutes and
then decided to forget it all. Shane suggested they walk

downtown and enjoy all that Sweetfern Harbor had to offer. By the time they reached Morning Sun Coffee, an hour had passed since Daniel's arrest. That was all the time it took for rumors to swirl around. Molly recognized the couple and approached them. She took their orders and Sandra asked how rumors flew around so fast.

"I've never known that answer, but in this town, it never takes long. Someone probably saw him being taken from the bed and breakfast or maybe recognized him in the police car as it drove by and drew their own conclusions. I guess that confirms Patrick Anderson was murdered. I mean, I still thought it could have been an accidental drowning, but apparently not." Molly took their orders and smiled at them ruefully. "Sorry you folks had to get a front row seat to all of this. Sweetfern Harbor really is a wonderful little town."

Sandra looked onto the street. The town was picturesque and if one didn't know about the crime, one would simply see it as a peaceful little village. Several more customers arrived. The Dickinsons talked about their afternoon plans. Shane suggested they have Jon take them out on a sailboat if he could fit them into his schedule.

Sweetfern Harbor residents had something new to talk about, but it didn't mar the hospitality shown to all visitors. Sandra and Shane paid the tab and left for Jonathan Wright's boat business, determined to make the best of the remainder of their visit.

Daniel Swift slumped in his chair facing Detective Rivers and Chief Ingram.

"If you won't tell us how you killed him, at least tell us how you knew Patrick Anderson," Mac said.

Daniel jerked his head up. He had called his lawyer, who advised him to say nothing until he arrived. Christopher O'Malley was an hour away, however, and the police had been relentless in their questioning. Daniel knew he should follow Christopher's advice, but he wanted to prove his innocence and get the interrogation over with. He was convinced he could simply give them the facts and walk away free and innocent. When Mac asked the first question, he was thrown off-guard. Without thinking of the consequences, he decided to answer.

"All right, if you'll stop harassing me, I'll tell you how I knew him. We were in college together. And let me tell you, no disrespect to the dead, but Patrick Anderson was a horrible guy, and not just that – he was a thief. I don't mean he stole little things. Patrick stole my identity. Twice. He stole everything that meant anything to me. He worked in the records office of the university. He found my file and used everything as his own – awards, academics, the works. He came from a wealthy family, his dad's family were all doctors. He was no star student and wanted to get his parents off his back so he could go back to partying."

Daniel's scowl deepened with anger. "He took my good grades and honors and doctored them so his name was on top and inserted them into his file. His poor academics became mine, thanks to Patrick's total lack of anything resembling ethics." He shuffled his feet and tried to cross his ankle over one knee. The shackles on his ankles prevented him from doing that easily. He settled back in his chair again. "It took years for me to get my rightful reputation back."

"How did you know he was going to be in Sweetfern Harbor this weekend, and specifically at Sheffield Bed and Breakfast?" Mac kept his eyes on the suspect.

"I didn't know that at all. Believe me, it was an unpleasant surprise. Two unpleasant surprises, in fact. One was Patrick Anderson, the guy who tried to ruin my academic career, and the other was Alexandra Cornell, the woman who tried to ruin my life by stalking me for years. I almost left that night but then decided to...take care of matters once and for all."

"And so you managed to drown a fitness buff like Patrick, all on your own?" Mac said.

"I didn't – you know what? I don't have anything else to say until my lawyer gets here."

The detective signaled the officer to take Daniel back to his cell.

"There is no way he managed to kill Patrick by himself. From all accounts, Patrick was an expert in the water," Mac said. "If Daniel went out there to kill him, wouldn't Patrick have been good enough to swim farther out? Or head toward the shore?"

"Maybe he took him by surprise somehow," Brenda offered, though she was not convinced either.

"There had to have been two perpetrators out there. I'm not even sure he was the one anyway. His words and body language rang totally false. Why does he care so much about having a lawyer?"

"I saw the body. Patrick looked strong enough to fight off one person for sure," Chief Ingram said.

"I don't expect to get much more from him once his attorney gets here. We'll have to be strategic." Mac updated Brenda and after discussion, they both felt Daniel was concealing something.

Carrie Porter chatted with Allie. "We love this little town so much," she said. "Are there any out-of-the-way spots around here where we can take a picnic lunch? Rick is showing a rare romantic streak this weekend and I'm not going to let this opportunity pass us by."

This was the time for Allie to shine. She loved to show off her local knowledge. "I'll have the chef prepare box lunches for you. There is a perfect spot I can tell you about." Allie started to give directions to a secluded beach area.

"That sounds perfect, but are there any other spots? He'll probably want several suggestions, so we can choose."

Allie jotted down a few possibilities situated near town but still secluded and passed the list to Carrie. "Did you take a look at the box lunch menu? Do you have any objections?"

"We looked at the menu. It's fine. Can you throw in a bottle of red wine? No preference on which one, just something not too acidic."

They completed the plans and Allie left to talk with Chef Pierre. When Allie found Carrie again, she told the guest the picnic lunch would be ready in fifteen minutes. The couple headed toward their car in the parking lot to pack a few things.

"Which spot have you chosen, Rick?" Carrie asked.

"None of them," he said. She noted teasing in his eyes. "No one has to know where we're really going. I have the perfect spot picked out already, and it's not on that list."

Carrie basked in his jovial mood. They rarely had this much time to enjoy one another away from their work at the hospital. She planned to take full advantage of the day alone with him. They drove a few miles and Carrie soaked up the beauty all around them.

"How far is it?" she asked.

"We'll be there in about an hour. I'll give you a hint. It's a wildlife refuge."

"I hope there aren't wild animals out here. Am I going to have to ride a moose to the picnic areas?"

"There are woods, and water, but no moose, I'm afraid. One more hint…you've never been out in a canoe, so I thought this could be your first adventure in one. How about that?"

"I'm game for anything on water. I can't wait to see where it is." She smiled adoringly at him.

Rick began to relax the longer he drove. His idea had been perfectly thought out and planned. It was a good way to get Carrie away from other people and it gave him relief, too. He toyed with the idea of spending the entire day and that night in the area where they were headed, which offered cabins for rent. Neither had signed up for dinner at Sheffield Bed and Breakfast, so no one would expect them to be there. He broached the idea to Carrie. She thought it was a great plan.

"Let's see how much we like the area first. If the cabins are too rustic, I may want to head back to the bed and breakfast. You know how I like my comforts. I'm not a fan of any wild animals, for that matter."

"I know, but this could be fun," he pressed, taking a fast curve on the highway.

"We'll see."

Carrie was surprised and enthralled with the beauty of the refuge park when they arrived. No one was in sight except for the conservation ranger who greeted them.

"A few people are booked in some of the cabins. Most are here for privacy and the park is large and quite isolated, so you should enjoy a quiet time." He smiled at them while he pointed out various things of interest in the sanctuary. They thanked him and drove forward.

"I feel like we are hundreds of miles from civilization," Carrie said, gazing out at the towering trees with sunlight filtering down.

"It does feel that way. No nosy proprietors bugging us about our plans for the day…no pagers buzzing us from the hospital…"

"Rick, I thought we agreed not to talk about work," Carrie reproached him.

He apologized and instead watched the green woods around them give way to a lush marshland as they approached the picnic area. Rick parked the car near a pavilion where they sat and enjoyed the packed lunch. Carrie noted that Rick's eyes never seemed to stop roaming the landscape. His leg jiggled under the table as he bounced his knee up and down.

"What's the matter?"

"This wine's no good. Too acidic for me," Rick said, distracted. "How about we head for that little supply post by the rental cabins that the ranger told us about?" Carrie agreed when he pointed out that they would have to walk that direction to get to the rental canoes anyway, and their picnic lunch came to a swift end as they disposed of their trash and set off down the pathway.

Detective Rivers was informed when the lawyer Christopher O'Malley arrived and entered to confer with his client Daniel Swift. Mac hoped the attorney would encourage Daniel to tell what he knew. If he hadn't been a part of the crime, he may have seen it happen or know who did commit the murder. Mac looked at the clock and sighed with frustration. He needed a break. When he called Brenda, she told him all the guests were taken care of. She was free to meet him and enjoy time away for a while. They decided to meet at Sweet Treats. It was mid-afternoon, and both had a sweet tooth. Mac arrived before she did.

"Hello, Mac, do you want your favorite?" Hope started to pull a tray from the glass cabinet.

"I'll wait for Brenda. In the meantime, how about a cup of strong coffee?"

"It's that kind of day, is it?" Hope Williams poured a

mug of coffee and asked Mac how the investigation was going.

"As well as can be expected. Right now, we are getting close to someone, but he's got his attorney down there so I'm not sure how fast we'll be able to move on it."

Hope didn't press for details, knowing they were not coming anyway. She respected Mac Rivers and was happy he and Brenda worked together on cases. When Brenda walked in, Hope offered her a hot beverage as well.

"I'll take coffee." Brenda's eyes popped when she perused the display of fresh pastries. "And…I'll take a slice of the lemon pound cake with a dollop of whipped cream."

"I'm going for the chocolate cake," Mac said. They chatted while Hope prepared their plates. "Let's find a spot away from the window, Brenda. I'd just as soon not know what's going on outside right now."

Brenda and Mac knew without saying that their conversation would be about the murder of Patrick Anderson. That was another reason to head for a table apart from the others. Hope's shop had room for five bistro tables. Most of her customers bought sweets by the dozen and left.

"I know that if Daniel killed Patrick, he didn't do it alone," Mac said. "I was hoping he'd waive his right to a lawyer, or ask for a plea bargain and tell us the whole story."

Brenda chuckled. "How often does that happen?" She forked a piece of cake. "When Alexandra mentioned seeing Daniel down there, she was completely lucid. She wasn't going crazy like you witnessed. I think she has sane moments and that was one of them. She mentioned she saw the body being put in the box, as she called it. I can't believe she let that slip but when I asked her what else she saw, she clammed up again. She resents Daniel right now because he let her know he's not interested in renewing their relationship. I can see why, now that I've seen this other side to Alexandra. She seems delusional, Mac. It worries me."

"She may have fingered him for the crime as a part of this delusional thinking. Perhaps she wanted him to squirm. I hope she isn't lying."

"Did he balk when you asked him about Patrick?"

"He seemed surprised we knew they were acquainted."

"When this is all over, let's go sailing on the ocean, Mac. A nice long cruise in the salt air will heal us."

"Until the next crisis," he said. "Crime never sleeps."

"Good thing the Sweetfern Harbor police don't sleep, either," she grinned.

He smiled in agreement and swallowed the last of the coffee. He kissed Brenda before he left, and she said she was headed back to the bed and breakfast.

Mac headed straight for the police station, his steps swift and sure. He was determined to get some answers about the case and thought about the different avenues of investigation he still wished to pursue. "Detective," the clerk said as he entered, "Christopher O'Malley wants to talk with you and the chief. I got word from one of the officers down the hall."

Mac's steps picked up. He thought O'Malley must be ready to make some kind of deal. He stopped at the chief's office to tell him. He turned when he heard Brenda's voice calling after him.

"You forgot your keys, Mac. I found them on our table after I stayed to chat a bit longer with Hope, but you were way ahead of me."

"You could have called me, Brenda." He filled her in on the latest. She was eager to be in on the meeting.

Chief Ingram introduced Brenda to Christopher and explained her role with the police department. He also mentioned she owned Sheffield Bed and Breakfast where his client and the homicide victim had both booked a stay for the weekend. Christopher did not look terribly pleased to hear all of this, but his demeanor remained congenial, as if they were conducting a social meeting.

"My client only wants to tell his side of the story. He has information that may help your case. He wants leniency in exchange for his information, and immunity against certain charges…"

Mac forced the sarcastic laugh back into his throat. Brenda stared at the attorney. "What kind of charges?" she asked.

"What exactly does he mean by leniency?" Mac said, regaining his voice with some consternation.

The attorney quickly realized Mac was less sympathetic and focused on Brenda. "Just charges of misdemeanors, failure to report crimes, that sort of thing. He doesn't want to be charged as an accessory after the fact." Christopher sighed and leaned in a little bit. "He's promised me it isn't anything bad. He just wants any sentencing reduced to parole only, if he's charged with anything at all." Brenda contemplated this but ultimately it was up to the chief of police. She turned to look at Bob.

Chief Ingram shifted forward. "We would like to have his confession, but I'll confer with the judge and my detective, as well as the officers involved. He's asking for something he probably won't be granted. There's no immunity granted without us hearing what he's got, that's for sure. Let's be clear on one thing, Mr. O'Malley. Murder means a death sentence. If he gets a life sentence, it will be with no possibility of parole."

Christopher's face grew hard. "You are presuming he is the murderer. He isn't. You should be looking at hard evidence. The judge is going to rake you and your team over the coals—"

"Have it your way," Mac interrupted the lawyer. Christopher abruptly shut his mouth and stood up straighter. Mac knew this wasn't the first time an outside lawyer had misinterpreted the way small-town law enforcement worked, but Mac didn't offer that observation aloud.

After Christopher left the office, Mac took a deep breath and rubbed his forehead. "He's a jerk, but he's right about evidence. We have one unpredictable witness and nothing else."

"We still have the DNA results from samples lifted from the body and inside the footlocker," Brenda said. "Once that comes back, we might have real evidence." Even as she said it, Brenda felt it was all in vain. She gazed out into the hallway where Christopher O'Malley had recently stormed out. "I find it hard to believe his lawyer is asking for a deal."

"It's early in the game," Mac said. "It's just jockeying for power. This tells me we have the right man. We just have to make sure he tells us what we need to know. We need to find who helped out."

Brenda shook her head. "I'm not so sure."

7

REVISED CONFESSIONS

Brenda and Mac looked forward to dinner with their bed and breakfast guests that evening. Most planned to leave the following day, though several opted to remain a few days longer, hoping the cloudy weather would blow over and bring more sunshine to enjoy along the coast.

As Brenda came out of the kitchen, she saw Allie at the front desk and invited her to join the dinner that night. Brenda liked to have some of her employees socialize with her guests at meals sometimes. "It's grilled steak tonight. Pierre's specialty," Brenda said with a smile.

"That sounds delicious. I can't wait," Allie said, her eyes round with excitement for the special meal. It was good to focus on things like this after such a long and frustrating investigation, Brenda reflected. "Don't look so sad, Brenda. It's working so well," Allie commented in confusion. When Brenda asked her what she meant, Allie continued, "The new chef. He's doing great, isn't he? What's the problem?"

Brenda realized the misunderstanding and sighed. "It's not that...you're right, Allie. Chef Pierre has been a fantastic chef while Morgan's on the honeymoon and everyone is drooling over his creations, not just you. Morgan and Tim have ten more days before they return. By then, if Morgan still wants to give up her job, I think we know who our next chef will be." She smiled at Allie and the young reservationist's sunny demeanor returned.

At dinner that night, Allie sat next to Alexandra and across from the Dickinsons. Sandra wondered aloud about the absence of Rick and Carrie.

"They decided not to sign in for dinner. They went on an outing today," Allie said. "She told me they weren't sure if they would be back in time for dinner. They took a sweet little box lunch picnic up the coast...Carrie was so excited! Rick was going to surprise her with a location, so I gave them several suggestions when she asked me. Little secluded nooks, perfect for time alone. Maybe he's going to propose or something!" Allie winked and turned to Alexandra right next to her and gushed, "Isn't that just so romantic?"

Alexandra turned red just then and suddenly coughed as if choking. Brenda jumped up from her chair to help dislodge whatever she swallowed. After a few pats on Alexandra's back, the woman shook her head and held her hand up signaling she was fine.

"I suppose I didn't chew that bite of steak well enough. I'm fine." She turned to Allie. "Did you say they wanted to be alone?" Allie said yes. Alexandra toyed with her fork for a moment, her eyes down. "I think they're running away," Alexandra said in a subdued tone.

Mac perked up at her comment. "Why would that be?"

"If I committed a crime, I'd run away before anyone realized I wasn't so perfect after all."

Brenda sensed the change in Alexandra's demeanor and quickly changed the subject. She asked how the others spent their day. She didn't miss the sly, conspiratorial look Alexandra threw her.

Conversations ebbed and flowed about guests' various outings. Sandra found herself eyeing Alexandra more than once. The woman didn't say anything else and enjoyed her meal in silence as if she hadn't made such a bombshell of a comment. It was a terrible accusation and Sandra wondered why Brenda and Mac had let it pass so easily. She felt more reassured when the dinner guests began to leave for tea and drinks and desserts in the sitting room and Brenda asked Alexandra to stay behind a moment with her and Mac. Sandra marched out of the room to get her usual chamomile tea with a righteous smile on her face.

"Let's have our dessert here at the table if you don't mind," Brenda said to Alexandra when the three of them were alone in the dining room. "I have a special cheesecake tartelette I'd love to share with you." Brenda served her guest a small plate of berry-topped tarts dusted with sugar.

"I would love that. In fact, Brenda, this is a good opportunity for us to chat," Alexandra said in a mild tone as she took her dessert plate. "There is another chapter I'm ready to reveal to you. Do you want to hear the whole story?"

Brenda knew it had to be about Patrick's death. "It's what we've been waiting to hear, Alexandra. We're all ears." Mac kept his focus on Alexandra as he spoke. She agreed he was right, though she did not quite meet his eyes and moved the dessert around on her plate a bit like a child playing with her food. Mac cleared his throat to get her attention. "No more games, okay? I'd like to record this conversation and want you to understand this is an official interview. I'll have to say that on the recording. Do you mind if I do that?"

"I don't mind at all. I have to tell everything before I go completely mad." Mac set up his digital recording and spoke the date and time and then recited the names of the people present as he closed the hallway door and the one that led to the sitting room. He began. "Do you wish to have an attorney present?" Alexandra declined.

She began. "I had nothing to do with killing him. But that doesn't mean I don't know what happened. I know what I saw with my own eyes. I can even tell you what song the ukulele player was playing while it happened. I was listening to that lovely music and watching a man's murder, all at the same time. Later I had to try to forget everything, drown it in more mai tais than I can count, but for those few minutes, I lived in two worlds." Her eyes were far away and she gazed out the dining room windows to the gardens and the ocean beyond.

Brenda made a mental note of that comment, realizing they could perhaps use any video recordings of the wedding to figure out when the murder took place, based on when the ukulele player was playing specific songs. It still seemed like a tiny detail, however, when Alexandra was holding onto much more important information. "Tell us what you saw, Alexandra."

"I sat on the wall at first. I went there to enjoy the ocean as the sun went down and to listen to the music. It was all so beautiful – the dancing, the wedding guests toasting with champagne, Patrick swimming in the Atlantic that was spread out like a picture below me – and then I saw two men carrying a large trunk down to the shore. By then, the light was truly gone, and stars started to come out. I only saw them by the little light that shone from the streetlights and house lights nearby. One of the men carried a little rolling thing – a dolly, a wheeled cart. Then they both sat on the sand and watched Patrick swim. At first I thought they were simply there to observe the beauty like I was doing…" She trailed off, looking away from the outside view. "But then they stood up. I saw it was Daniel and Rick. It shocked me. They called to Patrick and their voices were friendly at first. Like perhaps they wanted to take a swim with him. He yelled and gestured back to them that the water was fine and challenged them to jump in." Alexandra twisted her fingers together.

"Patrick was always egging someone on. He liked taunting people. The two men stripped off their outer clothes and waded out and then began swimming toward him. He must have asked them about the box because they turned a little and seemed to be explaining it to him or at least talking about it. I couldn't hear them by that time. The ukulele player was playing such a lovely song just then…"

"What happened next? Down in the water, I mean?" Brenda asked. Alexandra was trailing off, thinking back. Brenda didn't want her to lose her train of thought now.

"They swam a few strokes around him and then in a flash Daniel locked an arm around Patrick's neck while Rick wrenched his wrists back behind him. Both were surrounding Patrick, behind him, above him, and together they pushed him under the water. At first I thought it was one of those stupid games boys play in the water – but then I saw Daniel and Rick fight against him harder and harder, holding him under. A long time. Too long. And then finally there was no more thrashing around in the water and Patrick went completely still." She shuddered and curled into herself at the memory.

"Do you want something to drink, Alexandra?" Brenda asked. She said yes, and Brenda poured ice water from the pitcher on the buffet. She sipped it twice and resumed.

"They dragged his body out of the water up onto the sand. It was an ugly thing. Worse than watching them drown him. It took them two tries before they managed to put him into the box. His limbs kept bending in the wrong directions, or his hand would get stuck. They didn't care how they shoved him in there to fit. I thought I was going to be sick. Just when I thought the whole thing was over, I saw Rick grab his tie from his clothes on the sand and sling it around Patrick's neck. He pulled hard. Maybe Patrick hadn't been dead after all? I suppose he was making sure. Can you imagine, waking up after your own drowning, your body contorted and bruised, only to be strangled to death?" She looked up at Brenda with huge, pale eyes. "I'll never forget that sight."

Brenda was at a loss for words. Among Alexandra's quirks was a habit of imagining herself to be in a horrible situation, complete with morbid detail. It was unusual, to say the least.

Then, oddly, Alexandra grinned at them. "That's why Rick is running away. He isn't such a romantic as he wants people to think."

"What did Rick have against Patrick?" Mac asked.

"I don't know. I didn't know him until I met him here. I know Patrick came from a very wealthy family. I think his father was the chief of medicine at some well-known hospital, I don't know where. I heard later Patrick was a bigwig in a hospital, too." She frowned. "I know he never became a doctor. He wasn't that smart. Doesn't Rick work in a hospital? I don't know, maybe they knew each other from somewhere else. All I know is from what I saw, I would never let myself be taken on a 'romantic picnic' with a man like that. And to think, all this time, I thought Daniel was the one for me…"

Brenda asked Alexandra to keep what she told them to herself. "You've done a brave thing, sharing all this with us. I know you've been carrying quite a burden with you."

Alexandra warmed at the empathy flooding Brenda's eyes. "I think I'll feel better after this. It is good to finally say what I saw. I felt safer telling it all now that I know Daniel will be locked up."

"Did he threaten you?" Mac asked. "Does he know that you were a witness?" He needed even a hint of evidence to keep the man behind bars until they could gather hard evidence from the DNA.

"He didn't say anything in particular, but he scared

me. I promised I wouldn't say anything once…but it was strange. I realized he didn't even know I had seen him and Rick that night. When he figured it out, it was hard to miss his anger."

That night, Alexandra slept better than she had for a long time, especially once Mac and Brenda assured her that they would send out an all-points bulletin to look for Rick and Carrie in case Carrie was in any danger being alone with him.

Brenda and Mac talked long into the night and figured out their next moves.

The next morning shed new light on everything. Brenda woke up with a good feeling, and sure enough, over breakfast a technician from the evidence processing lab called Mac's mobile phone with the good news that they had found positive proof of ownership of the footlocker.

"We searched every pocket and hidden crevice in it. We found an ink print that had been made by a wet receipt on the inside lining of the trunk and were able to reverse-image it. It came from a nearby thrift store. The trunk was purchased secondhand just this week. The receipt was paid in cash so there was no name on it, but we were able to requisition the cash receipts book from that thrift store and guess what – the carbon copy in the receipt book turned up positive for prints matching the ones you took from your suspects, Rick Dawson and Daniel Swift."

Mac and Brenda jumped in the car and immediately went to the police station for a new round of interrogations using the latest evidence.

When Christopher O'Malley accompanied his client

into the interrogation room, Mac told him they were ready to listen to what he had to say. He promised no deal, knowing that the police already held the most important information.

Christopher said, "My client is innocent. Mr. Swift knows who killed Patrick Anderson."

"We already have that information, as it turns out. There's an APB out to bring that suspect in."

Daniel slumped back in his chair, a little shocked, and realized his chance to make a deal had passed. He wished he had never agreed to help Rick at the thrift store that day and regretted being a witness to Patrick taking his last breath. He gritted his teeth visualizing Alexandra's face around every corner, smiling placidly with revenge.

The attorney glanced at his client. The distress on Daniel's face was one he sometimes recognized in others he represented. This man looked as if ready to explode. Christopher assured him he would be found innocent and cautioned him not to say anything hasty. However, Daniel had endured too much.

"That woman is out of her mind," Daniel exploded. "Don't you see? Alexandra is trying to frame me. That's what she told you, right? If she told you I killed Patrick, she lied to you."

"What does Alexandra have to do with it?" Brenda said.

"Alexandra Cornell has stalked me for years, ever since our breakup. I was lucky to get away from her the first time, but she has plagued my life ever since. I bet she told you stories about me that aren't true. Whatever she saw, or says she saw, you shouldn't believe it." They waited and watched the suspect, whose knee shook under the table with impatience.

The police officers had not yet contradicted him, and this was a sign to Daniel that perhaps he had hope. "She's like a vampire, she leeches drama and attention when something doesn't go her way. She's playing you! Her mother was mentally ill – she murdered Alexandra's brother and then committed suicide. It runs in her family."

"What makes you think Alexandra told us she saw something?" Mac said.

"My client has nothing more to say," Christopher interrupted.

Daniel held up his hand. "I have plenty to say. She's no innocent witness. I'm done waiting around for someone else to do the right thing, so I'll tell you what really happened." He leaned into the table, closer to the detectives. "She helped drown Patrick. I saw it happen."

Even Brenda gasped.

"She looks weak, but she is almost as strong as Patrick was. Those fingers of hers can hold on tight as death. Ask me how I know," he said bitterly, rubbing one arm as if remembering something from long ago. "She and Rick planned it well. They even got me involved in a stupid way – Rick strong-armed me into helping him carry that big footlocker around that he found at the thrift store. I'm sure he was just trying to get my fingerprints on something."

Brenda felt light-headed and excused herself, leaving Mac to finish up with the story Daniel related. It was true they had found nothing to pin the murder directly on Daniel. Alexandra was the only link placing him at the crime scene. Rick and Carrie, long gone, were even more important to find now, but first Brenda told Officer Sims and Officer Thompson to find and arrest Alexandra Cornell.

Brenda went into Mac's office and called Allie. "Can you text me a list of the areas you told Carrie Porter about? We're trying to locate them, and the APB hasn't turned up anything yet. We're going to need all the help we can get right now." Mac appeared in the doorway and mouthed more instructions to her just then. "Mac said if they come back to the bed and breakfast, call us right away. Keep your winsome personality going in front of them, Allie. Just don't let them think anything is wrong."

Allie Williams hung up, puzzled. She had no idea what was wrong, but then recalled Alexandra's remark during dinner about the couple's picnic excursion being an attempt to run away. Allie was ready to play any part necessary.

"That's strange," Phyllis said, coming downstairs just then. Allie asked what she meant. "I just went into clean with my staff and Rick's and Carrie's room is empty. Did they check out early?"

Allie told her about the conversation just then with Brenda, and about what Alexandra had said the night before during dinner. "I guess Alexandra knew what she was talking about." The young reservationist scattered a few notes aside on her desk until she found the list of the four secluded spots she had suggested to Carrie. She quickly texted the list to Brenda.

Brenda checked the list of locations and started to mentally map them out. Back in Mac's office, she told him most of the suggestions were within a ten-mile radius of Sweetfern Harbor. "Do we add these locations to the APB? What if they didn't even go to any of these places?"

"They could be anywhere, but they still have to come back to pick up their belongings at the bed and breakfast," Mac said.

Brenda's mobile rang and she answered the call from Phyllis. When she hung up, she told Mac that Rick Dawson and Carrie Porter would not be returning to Sheffield Bed and Breakfast any time soon. "There goes that hope," she said. Mac suggested they check in with the chief of police on the status of the larger search.

Chief Ingram filled them in on what he had so far. "Patrick's parents are in Europe and on their way back to the states. His father is a well-known physician and oddly, he didn't seem all that shaken up over his son's death. Maybe he's just a quiet person, though. I didn't speak with the mother. The doctor was hard to figure out, but he could be in shock." Bob worried about Carrie Porter too, and they resolved that finding Carrie and Rick needed to be the top priority. It wasn't only a murderer they had to track down; it could be they needed to prevent him from taking another victim.

Carrie basked in the sunshine bathing the canoe while Rick paddled along. They were near the edge of the water and Rick was quiet, deep in thought.

"This is so lovely. We should have come straight here, not to Sweetfern Harbor," Carrie mused, trailing her fingers in the water. "That man's murder was such a downer…"

He looked at her sharply. "Why do you have to be so negative, Carrie? You know what…it's sad how often this happens. It's worse because it just reminds me of the first time you doubted me."

Carrie sat up straighter, her romantic mood turned sour. "Rick, that is all in the past. How was I to know such devastating lies were being told about you? It was so long ago. We hadn't known each other very long. I know it was a horrible time for you, and I'm sorry, but is it truly worth getting so upset over? Honestly, I didn't mean to bring it up, I just meant—"

"I almost lost my license over it," Rick said vehemently, the paddle forgotten in his lap for the moment. "How can you just dismiss it like that? It took a long time and more money than I care to remember to fight those court cases." He gave a short, bitter laugh. "I couldn't believe it when I saw him at Sheffield Bed and Breakfast. He had the nerve to act at first as if he didn't recognize me." The bitter laugh escaped his throat again. "He hurt plenty of people, even that young woman Alexandra. I talked to her about it just the other day."

Carrie worried about Rick's change in mood and his mention of the woman at the bed and breakfast, but didn't ask what he was talking about. That would have to come later. She sat quiet and tense in her canoe seat. Rick's morose expression startled her into remembrance of the ugly past. Rick had been accused of intentionally causing the deaths of patients on the operating table, at a time when the couple had known one another for less than a year.

As a young nurse, Carrie had fallen deeply in love with the handsome young anesthesiologist, who took her on dates hiking and to historic sites around the state. She felt like they were a perfect match. His thick dark hair curled when he let it grow long and all the nurses secretly swooned over his good looks, but for Carrie, it was Rick's deep brown eyes that reached to her very soul.

She recalled how shaken she had been when rumor swirled around Rick about the malpractice lawsuits and investigations about the two deaths during surgeries. Eventually he had been cleared in the matter, but it remained a bitter stain that he carried with him and it seemed to dog him like a curse, popping up at unexpected times, tainting their time together when he reproached her for not believing him at first.

She decided the best course of action was to focus on the present time. "Think about this place – it's got to be the most beautiful wildlife refuge I've ever seen. You always pick the perfect places to bring me. And even though you love being on vacation, don't pretend you don't like being every surgeon's favorite anesthesiologist. You have a gift, Rick."

Rick's smile didn't reach his eyes. He looked at Carrie and held his gaze on her, seeming to contemplate more than he could put into words. Yet she was not certain that all of the thoughts he held back were good ones.

She was grateful when he focused again on the canoe. Rick paddled them back toward land and even reached over to hold Carrie's hand as they coasted a little through a pretty stretch of shady trees overhanging the edge of the water. "You can now say you have gone canoeing, Carrie. How was it?"

"It's great, especially since I have a big strong boyfriend to do all the paddling," she teased, trying to get him to smile. "Maybe next time we can take a sailboat and both work the ropes, or a motor boat so we can go fast and you can rest those biceps." She patted the bunched muscles of his upper arm where he held the paddle in the water and inwardly breathed a sigh of relief when she saw his face relax.

"Maybe we should rent a cabin tonight? The one we passed looked vacant." She wanted to prolong the time with Rick and see if she could coax any more smiles out of him. Carrie planned to use that night to their advantage, and in the solitude and peaceful wilderness, she knew she would feel closer to Rick than ever before.

The next morning, Carrie awakened to birds singing in the wooded area behind the cabin. She ran her hand over the side where she expected to touch Rick. The sheets were cool. The small kitchen in the corner featured a coffee maker, and when she sat up in bed, she saw Rick had brewed some for them both. She got up to pour a cup. She looked out the windows and glimpsed no sign of him. She wished he had waited for her to go hiking with him. She curled up against the generous pillows and drank the hot beverage. Fifteen minutes passed. She rinsed the cup and headed for the shower. She knew Rick would want a turn in the shower after his hike.

Refreshed, Carrie emerged clean and dressed from the steamy little bathroom, excited to talk to Rick about the day ahead. Yet Rick was nowhere in the cabin. She walked onto the small front porch and shielded her eyes from the morning sun and searched for him. The woods and marshy places around were quiet except for birdsong and the scurrying small animals who hunted for their breakfasts. She knew he was out walking somewhere because their car was still parked where it had been the day before. With a sudden flash of insight, she grabbed her car keys and drove down the road to the tiny store, certain she would find Rick in friendly conversation with the clerk or perhaps some fellow hikers and explorers.

The little store itself was small and empty of people, save for the clerk. "Have you seen a man in his forties come in here this morning?" The older man behind the counter adjusted his glasses and smiled at her. "He has dark hair and brown eyes," she said.

"A young family came in for a few things when I opened at seven. Two young hikers replenished their supplies…let's see…the only other person has been the park ranger. He stops in for coffee and the latest news. Maybe you can ask him if he's seen your husband."

"Oh, he's not my…he's just my boyfriend." She didn't like explaining this to strangers and a blush spread on her cheeks beneath the worry wrinkling her forehead.

He noted the look on Carrie's face. "He probably just went out hiking in the lowlands. Those hiking loops go out some eight or ten miles. I'm sure he'll be back by lunch."

"Are there wild animals out there?"

The man chuckled good-naturedly. "Only the cute little fuzzy kind, I can assure you. We're too far away from the mountains to get little black bears and bobcats and whatnot. Don't worry about him. He probably lost track of time. I'll keep a lookout and send him your way." Carrie told him their cabin number and gave him her cell number.

Carrie purchased a few snacks and took them with her to the car. She loaded the grocery bag in the trunk and gasped when she looked inside. When had Rick loaded all their things from the bed and breakfast into the car? She recalled he had been upstairs while she talked with Allie. Perhaps he took the luggage down the back stairs. As much as she wanted to believe this was a sign that he planned to make further romantic gestures at their cozy little cabin in the woods, a bad feeling rushed through her stomach and made her knees go weak with dread.

She drove back to the cabin and rushed into the small bedroom. When she opened the closet, she was relieved to see that Rick's small suitcase remained on the floor. Then, for the first time, she noticed an envelope on the nightstand on Rick's side of the bed. Carrie tore it open.

Dear Carrie, I love you with all my heart, but I must release you. You do not understand what I struggle with right now, so I must write it down before I go. I suppose you did not even recognize the man who almost ruined me all those years ago… after all, he had longer hair back then and looked more like a hippie than someone in the position of CEO. Only Patrick Anderson's father could have pulled that off, putting his unqualified party-boy son in a position of power. Patrick picked me, for some reason known only to him, all to discredit me and he almost won. He almost destroyed my professional life. You saw that up close and yet I always sensed you never quite understood what I went through. Yesterday showed me just how far apart we truly are on the matter. As for me, I never forgot that ordeal and vowed one day to get my revenge. I've managed to do that…I've managed to free myself from that terrible past, but revenge comes at a great cost. I cannot go through years of courtrooms and trials again. I am leaving you our bank cards, plus cash and our credit cards. I can't tell you where I am going. Please don't look for me. All my love is for you and for the life we could have shared if only my past and my present had not been so ruined by Patrick. Love, Rick.

8

FINAL RESOLUTION

Carrie Porter no longer heard the sounds of nature. Her peace and tranquility shattered into dull shock when she read the last handwritten note she would ever receive from the love of her life.

How could she have been so clueless? She knew there was something familiar about Patrick Anderson, but he didn't look the same. Even back then she glimpsed him only on rare occasions. She had forgotten his name as well. She kicked herself for not realizing his last name was so familiar from the upper circles in the medical world at the hospital where they had all worked for so long. She simply hadn't made the connection.

Then there was Rick's ordeal. At the time, Carrie had distanced herself from him, uncertain about the outcome but most of all scared for her own professional future. Would she lose her job at the hospital if she sat in a courtroom to support her boyfriend against her own employer? It was an impossible choice, but it was still one she wished she could repair.

She threw her remaining belongings in her suitcase and dumped everything in the back seat. She swerved around and headed for the front gate and the main roads. She had to find Rick and make sure he was all right. He said he got his revenge at a terrible cost. Did that mean he had committed a crime? The unthinkable swirled in her gut like nausea, but she couldn't imagine him murdering Patrick. Carrie convinced herself he meant Patrick's death felt like revenge, even though Rick himself had nothing to do with it. Surely that was the truth of the matter.

Carrie steered onto the road leading to the highway when she saw the conservation ranger's sedan pull up, blocking her lane. She reluctantly came to a stop. He stepped out and waved her over.

"You'll have to stay here until the authorities arrive, Ms. Porter." He directed her to park near the ranger station. "Where is your husband?"

"He's not my husband. We've been together for many years but we've never..." she trailed off, tears beginning to gather at the corners of her eyes. "I don't know where he is. I've been looking for him all over the refuge. I'm on my way to search along the highways. He's on foot. What if he's been in an accident?" The ranger's face didn't budge. "I have to keep looking, please."

Carrie pushed the letter from Rick to the back of her mind. If she could just find him and confirm that he was innocent, then his ridiculous talk about escaping to an unknown location would be something she could worry about later. She had to find him first.

The park ranger was speaking into a walkie talkie and then she heard the sirens approaching. The ranger signaled her to stay in place and moments later her car was flanked by two patrol cars from Sweetfern Harbor. An officer asked her to get out of the car. When she reached for her purse, he told her to leave everything.

Carrie shook with fear, realizing the car was being searched for evidence. She didn't want to think Rick did anything wrong. Hadn't he said he didn't wish to go through the courts and a trial again? There was no way he would risk that again.

A female officer stood with her while the car was being searched. "Ma'am, are you all right? Have you been harmed by your boyfriend in any way? Threatened or intimidated?"

Carrie felt deeply confused, looking from the vehicle search to the kindly, concerned female officer next to her. "What? No, he hasn't harmed me. He's missing, I'm looking for him—"

"It looks like you're planning to flee. Why did you pack everything?" The male officer called out, having paused at the open trunk of the car while he directed his question at Carrie.

Carrie shook her head and gave a slight shrug of her shoulders. "I didn't do that. I'm not fleeing anything. I didn't even know everything was packed out of our room until a few minutes ago. We were going for a short getaway out here and then, I thought, back to Sheffield House. What's going on? Is he under suspicion of something? Why won't anyone tell me anything?"

The officer didn't answer. He resumed the search.

She turned slightly when she heard the female officer speaking in a hush with the park ranger. His voice was deeper and more audible than hers. "It's hard to read people these days. I'd never have thought that nice young couple was involved in what happened in Sweetfern Harbor..."

Carrie wanted to shout at him that they were not involved in anything. Instead, she swallowed hard and became aware this search had been going on for quite some time. Perhaps since she and Rick left the bed and breakfast. What did the police in Sweetfern Harbor know about Rick? She felt sick to her stomach as she waited for the search of her car to end, and the whole time, she pictured Rick on foot, fleeing farther and farther away from her.

Brenda was at her computer when word came from Mac that Carrie was en route to Sweetfern Harbor in a squad car and Rick Dawson was considered on the run. Brenda had time to finish up her research before Carrie arrived at the police station. She had found a series of articles dating back almost a decade regarding an interesting incident in Rick's anesthesiology career. He had been investigated by the hospital for improperly administering anesthesia to patients and causing the death of two individuals during surgery. The investigation had turned into a lawsuit and a counter-suit, a protracted series of courtroom battles as Rick claimed his innocence and tried to prove what had really happened, at times even arguing against the CEO of his own hospital. She did a double-take when she saw who that CEO had been.

Patrick Anderson, at age twenty-five, had longer hair back in those days, but in the courtroom photo she found online she recognized the same self-confident glint to his smile. He was described as unpopular with the staff, and one board member anonymously stated the inexperienced young man had been placed in the chief executive position by his famous father, who happened to be the chief physician and director of a large nearby hospital managed by the same company.

In testimony, Patrick Anderson described Rick Dawson as inept and careless, even though other witnesses described how Rick had obtained his degree with honors, held a spotless record until those two patient deaths, and seemed to be universally liked by his colleagues. Patrick had never even set foot in an operating room, but he seemed confident enough to pass judgment on the smallest details of Rick's work, once on the witness stand.

As Brenda continued reading, she understood why Rick's anger remained with him until Patrick's death. Rick Dawson spent years in and out of court, fighting lawsuits and appeals, both state and civil. If Patrick had been behind all of these lawsuits, obviously the Anderson family had spent a lot of money on lawyers to keep the fight going for quite some time. Rick even declared bankruptcy but at the last hour, he ultimately won his case and the hospital had been ordered to pay his remaining legal costs. His medical license was later reinstated, and his job restored, and a follow-up article from a few years later reported that Rick maintained a sterling reputation.

Nothing Brenda found explained why Patrick singled out Rick. Yet she felt this could be the key to breaking a confession wide open.

She closed her laptop and freshened up. When she walked the path from the cabin to her bed and breakfast, she met Phyllis and told her the latest.

"It's hard enough to believe Rick is guilty. But do you really think Carrie knew he did something like that?" Phyllis asked. "I do remember they grew rather quiet before taking their getaway. Do you think she knew and was in agreement that they had to run away?"

"I don't know." Brenda frowned. "I don't think she knew. Allie said she was very relaxed before they left. She talked a lot about how happy she was that Rick had thought of a romantic day together. I think she really did think that was his only plan. I'll know more when I hear her side of things." Phyllis asked how they got all the luggage out without Allie seeing it. "I think Rick must have done that while Carrie chatted with Allie. He could have easily taken it down the back stairs. I asked Chef Pierre if he saw any action like that go past the kitchen. He said he and his staff had been down in the wine cellar for a few hours taking inventory." She told Phyllis about Alexandra's involvement.

"Are you sure Daniel's telling the truth, that Alexandra helped kill Patrick? How do you know he and Alexandra aren't both lying?"

"I'm fairly sure he's telling the truth, but we'll know more detail soon. She's been arrested."

Phyllis almost asked to join Brenda at the police station, but several guests had checked out and there were rooms to deep clean and prepare for new arrivals. "Brenda, you go do what needs to be done. Don't you worry about the bed and breakfast, we will make sure everything is neat as a pin and running like clockwork."

Brenda smiled gratefully at her friend and headed for her car.

When she arrived, Brenda opted to park behind the police station. The yellow tape once cordoning off the back door where the footlocker had been found was now gone. She quickly found Mac and discussed all the findings and how the questioning should proceed.

"I think we need to know Carrie's role in all this," Brenda mused. "I think she was innocent. But if Rick and Carrie were together at the time he was in court back then over the lawsuits, there is no mention of her. I'm curious about when they met and how. He told me they'd been together for a long time, but he never mentioned anything about these court cases. I didn't see her in any of the pictures of the courtrooms, either. If they were together back then, wouldn't she have been sitting with him, supporting him?"

"If you think it's important and will help get her to acknowledge Rick's recent actions, go ahead and ask. But I don't see the relevance."

"The relevance is whether she knew he had been falsely accused by Patrick Anderson back then. If she was involved in that from the start, then maybe she shared Rick's animosity against him. In any case, she's been with Rick for years. That's plenty of time for him to tell her all about his past with Patrick."

Mac's door was open. He and Brenda looked up when

Officer Natalie Sims walked by with Carrie Porter. Carrie's face was ashen. She walked forward like a robot, her legs moving but nothing else betraying a ghost of her usual vibrancy.

"Let's go take a look at what they found in her vehicle before we talk to her," Mac said. They headed for the evidence room where the second officer set two bags down.

"We've impounded the car and still have to go over that," the officer said. "There is something we found in her purse that may interest you."

Mac and Brenda put gloves on and she took the envelope. Brenda read the note Rick wrote to Carrie aloud. "Wow. He admits getting revenge, though it's a little vague what he means. What do you think this 'great cost' means? And it does appear that Carrie had no idea he had committed any crime."

The detective asked the officer to make sure every law enforcement agency had a description of Rick Dawson.

"He has to be on foot," Brenda said. "He left the car for Carrie and there is no public transportation near the wildlife refuge, according to Officer Sims."

"Let's go have a talk with Carrie Porter," Mac said.

Mac asked if she wanted a lawyer present. "I don't know any lawyers. I suppose not." Carrie's eyes were wide and unblinking, and she still appeared to be in shock.

Brenda did not want to mention to the woman that they could get her a court-appointed lawyer after she was arrested. Technically Carrie was not even under arrest. She figured explaining the precarious situation would only make things worse. After voicing their initial planned questions, Brenda asked Carrie if Rick was a strong hiker.

"We have done a lot of hiking over the years. Why?"

"Do you think he has hiked up into the mountains? The White Mountains are only a couple days north of here, but there are other mountainous areas around here, too."

Tears edged beneath her thick eyelashes. Carrie's wavy blonde hair draped over her cheek before she pushed it back and blinked back the tears. "I don't know where he is. I don't know why he left, either. He was acting so odd yesterday…he kept talking about how Patrick almost ruined him years ago. I'm scared he did something drastic. Has anyone found him yet?" Neither Brenda nor Mac answered her, so she continued. "Anyway, it took Rick years to recoup from that court battle, he's never let it go. He managed to restore his good reputation at the hospital. I thought that was all that mattered."

"What was his reason for dredging it all up again?" Brenda asked.

"I didn't want to ask at that moment. It was our romantic getaway…I changed the subject and he was back to his old jovial self." She sniffed, and Brenda handed her a tissue. "I thought he had taken an early morning walk when I woke up this morning. When he didn't show up, I drove to the wildlife refuge's camp store and asked if he had been in there. No one had seen him. That's when I decided to search the roads, and that's when the park ranger pulled me over. Listen, Rick could be hurt. Someone needs to find him!"

"We'll find him," Mac said.

"Why can't I help? Am I under arrest? If I'm not under arrest, I want to leave."

"No. We don't have any reason right now to arrest you. Leave a contact number for us. We're keeping the note Rick left for you as evidence, also." Mac stood up. Carrie's eyes widened as she realized they had read the note. "Stay around town unless we say otherwise."

"If you want to keep your room at Sheffield Bed and Breakfast, you are welcome to remain until you are released to leave the area," Brenda said gently.

Carrie thought about this, clearly reluctant. She asked Brenda if she had to go down for meals. "I know word will get around that Rick is on the run. I want people to know that he just needs to get help," Carrie pleaded. "All the nightmares of the past hit him when he saw Patrick here."

"You certainly don't have to come down for meals, but you may find that socializing will help you cope. I certainly won't let anyone gossip," Brenda said.

Brenda told her she would take her back to the bed and breakfast. Mac said she should have her car back in a couple of days or so. Carrie had no option other than to go along with things the way they were now. She yearned for Rick.

In the car, Carrie asked Brenda if she thought Rick had anything to do with Patrick's death.

"I can't talk about the case with you, Carrie. Just know this much...there is evidence we don't have yet. We're expecting final results within twenty-four hours." She glanced at the woman next to her. "Hang in there. I'm sure things will work out for the best."

"I forgot that you are a police officer, too, Brenda."

Brenda explained her role with local law enforcement. "I've had investigative training and since Sheffield Bed and Breakfast is my first priority, I only come in on a case here and there."

She asked Carrie about her nursing career. By the time they reached the bed and breakfast, Brenda knew Carrie loved her job and loved working with her boyfriend. She also knew Carrie was likely only another minute or two away from collapsing in tears, so Brenda pulled into the rear driveway. They walked the pathway to the bed and breakfast and entered through the back door.

In the meantime, Mac decided to take Detective Bryce Jones with him to prod Daniel. After asking if he wanted his lawyer present, Daniel stated he was innocent and wanted to be set free.

Bryce and Mac sat across from him. "I want to hear every detail of what you saw happen," Mac said. "I find it hard to believe Alexandra managed to kill Patrick and then drag the box up the beach and get it into a car. Tell us what really happened."

"They had it on rollers. Surely you don't think she's stupid. The whole thing was planned out. Rick came up behind him in the water. Alexandra flirted with him and Patrick got distracted enough that he didn't hear Rick until it was too late. It was quite a fight, but Rick overpowered him."

"We didn't find any car tracks on the beach." Mac waited for that explanation.

"I told you, Alexandra is smart. She took low branches from the beach shrubbery and swept the tracks away."

"Did you and Rick know one another?" Bryce asked, changing tactics.

"We met after we checked in at Sheffield. He knew Patrick would be here, though I didn't. We got into a conversation when I told him I was so surprised to see someone from my past who almost ruined me. After talking in private I learned we had something in common when it came to Patrick Anderson. We both were hurt because Patrick got away with so much because of his family's status. I later saw Rick talking with Alexandra. You know, they left for walks twice that I know of."

Once Daniel Swift was released, Officer Sims caught Mac and Bryce in the hall. They were getting ready to go home.

"We just received word on Rick Dawson," she said. "He was less than five miles from the wildlife refuge."

"Call me as soon as he gets here," Mac said.

"That won't happen, Detective," Natalie said with a grim look. "He's on his way to the coroner's office. They found him hanging from a white oak in the wetlands." She gave details of the hangman's knot and the rope looped tightly over the limb of the majestic tree and the dead body dangling a few feet from the ground.

When Mac asked Brenda to convey the news to Carrie, it was the last thing she wanted to do. Brenda climbed the stairs of the bed and breakfast slowly to Carrie's room. When the guest let her in, she came in and sat on the bed next to her and gave her the news.

Fresh tears streamed down Carrie's face. "I knew it," she said between sobs, "why didn't I see? I could have helped him. He didn't want to go through that ordeal with the courtrooms again...but I could have helped him. I know he didn't murder anyone. But if he had only let me help him prove it. If only..."

For the moment, Brenda chose to let her believe whatever she wished. She waited until Carrie cried herself into a fatigue and then finally stretched across the bed, exhausted. Her eyelids closed. She drifted into a fitful sleep, twitching a little with nighttime interruptions, the same which would invade her nights for years to come.

Alexandra huddled on her bed in the corner of her cell. She sat with her knees drawn up at the corner where her hard cot met the cement walls and watched the tiny barred window in the door until she grew too exhausted to remain sitting and fell into a disturbed sleep. Her dreams roamed through Japan, her early childhood, happier times with her sweet young brother at her side, her mother only a distant shadow.

Early the next morning, she awoke, unrested and restless. Dreaming about the past was futile, she realized. There was too much about the present day crashing in upon her and she knew now what she needed to do. She accepted a cup of coffee, dry stale toast and an overcooked egg on a tray for breakfast and waited until her appointed time. At nine, she sat across from Brenda and Mac in the interrogation room. Her court-appointed lawyer, who was no help at all, sat next to her, and Officer Thompson stood by the door.

"Did you kill Patrick?" Brenda asked her. "How did you manage it?"

The lawyer tapped his client's arm. "You don't have to say anything."

Alexandra's smile lit the semi-darkened room. "I don't have to do anything. But I want to. I'm ready to tell them. Patrick's dead and I did it. He thought I was so weak, just some woman he could push around. He didn't know I had a hidden strength from all those years of workouts," she said, delicately flexing her hands against the edge of the table. "It proved to be my path to victory. You can release Daniel now. He's innocent. Now Daniel will see, I'm the one who saved him from a life of incarceration. Soon he and I will be together without interference from the likes of that awful Patrick."

Brenda chose to ignore the delusional assumptions. "How did you manage such a thing?"

"It was easy. Rick swam with me toward Patrick. I think he was surprised that we wanted to join him. As usual, he taunted me and asked why I was hanging out with Rick. Was I going to stalk Rick now? Where was Daniel? That kind of thing. I simply smiled and flirted with him. It didn't take much. I told him I'd been hoping he would just get jealous of my attentions to other men and try to hook up with me. Can you believe he fell for something like that? Me, going for Patrick? He was oblivious. He loved it. And he had no idea Rick was behind him, ready to headlock him and push him under water. I helped, you know. It isn't easy keeping such a strong swimmer subdued. He thrashed like a fish." Alexandra did not seem to think her words strange or disturbing at all. "But even a slippery fish can be subdued. It was two against one. Rick and I rolled him into the case. But then he woke up, and I realized even Rick was too weak for the job. I grabbed Rick's silk tie from the towel nearby and wrapped it around his neck. I heard something snap. I think it was his neck." She laughed sharply. "Yes, his neck cracked, I'm sure of it."

Thick silence filled the interrogation room. Mac shifted, not losing his composure. "Who decided to bring him here?"

"That was Rick's idea. He said the man had never paid for any of his crimes and it was time to dump him where he belonged. That was the best part of the whole thing." Her laugh pierced the small room again.

Her lawyer stopped everything at that point and asked to see a judge, to order a psychiatric evaluation before any further action in the case. Mac and Bob attempted to argue against it, claiming she had planned everything, but in the end, it proved fruitless and she was carted away to a locked mental ward for long-term treatment. Alexandra Cornell would never see the inside of a regular jail. Her DNA was on the tie, her fingerprints were on the footlocker, and there were two witnesses, but that would not be enough to convict the kind of woman capable of feigning such convincing, diabolical mental illness at times. She was mentally ill, they were convinced, but she was also sometimes faking it. That was the worst part.

Some days later, they sat in Mac's office discussing the case. "I guess all the loose ends are tied up now. Patrick's remains were retrieved by his family and the chief told me to officially close the case file." Mac offered Brenda a cup of fresh coffee. She accepted. They sat in silence, each thinking about the case. Brenda reached for a box of butter cookies and took one, offering the package to Mac.

"What a waste of lives," she said. "Patrick, Rick…I wonder what percentage of crimes are committed because of insanity."

"I have no idea." Mac stood and looked out the window. "Alexandra probably inherited her mental illness, but I don't know what possessed Rick Dawson to kill someone. Or himself, in the end. It's a sad end to the case, for sure."

"Hatred and resentment clouded Rick's judgment, I think. What Patrick did was awful, but Rick couldn't let it go. I guess that same resentment clouded Alexandra's life. Even Daniel's, to some extent," Brenda mused, taking the last bite of her cookie. "In the end, I guess it was Patrick who set everything in motion, though. He stole Daniel's identity, he pushed Daniel and Alexandra to break up, he went after Rick's career for no good reason. What drove Patrick to do all of that?"

"Privilege? The same rich jerk attitude he spread over everyone he met? Or maybe he was just immature and looking for power. We'll never know," Mac said, staring out at the golden cloud of sunset light spreading across the horizon. "But what I do know is that he can't do any more harm."

The light suffused the office through the windows and turned everything a beautiful shade of rosy gold and he turned to see his wife haloed in the light. He smiled at her.

"Speaking of harm, I've got to get away from these butter cookies, Mac. What do you say we take a walk down to the waterfront and go for that sailboat ride? I feel the need to breathe some fresh salt air."

Mac smiled at her warmly and reached over to take her hand. He told her that was a good idea. "Besides, it would be a crime not to take advantage of such a beautiful evening to look at my pretty wife, wouldn't it?"

Brenda's heart filled with love and affection for Mac as they strolled down the picturesque streets toward the water and the golden sunset beyond, hand in hand.

ABOUT THE AUTHOR

Wendy Meadows is the USA Today
bestselling author of many novels and
novellas, from cozy mysteries to
clean, sweet romances. Check out her
popular cozy mystery series
Sweetfern Harbor, Alaska Cozy and
Sweet Peach Bakery, just to name a few.

If you enjoyed this book, please take a few minutes to
leave a review. Authors truly appreciate this, and it helps
other readers decide if the book might be for them.
Thank you!

Get in touch with Wendy
www.wendymeadows.com

amazon.com/author/wendymeadows

goodreads.com/wendymeadows

bookbub.com/authors/wendy-meadows

facebook.com/AuthorWendyMeadows

twitter.com/wmeadowscozy

Made in the USA
Columbia, SC
09 February 2021